# Blind Passion

# Blind Passion
## A supernatural love affair

Malena Paltero

© Malena Paltero 2014 – All Rights Reserved.

Editing and cover design by: Writer Services, LLC
Book layout by: Chappell Graphix

ISBN 10: 1942389019
ISBN 13: 978-1-942389-01-9

Printed and bound in the United States of America

Prominent Books and the sunburst compass logo are Trademarks of Prominent Books, LLC

# TABLE OF CONTENTS

CHAPTER ONE ................................................................... 1
CHAPTER TWO ................................................................ 29
CHAPTER THREE ............................................................ 49
CHAPTER FOUR ............................................................... 77
CHAPTER FIVE ............................................................... 109
CHAPTER SIX ................................................................. 131
CHAPTER SEVEN ........................................................... 163
CHAPTER EIGHT ............................................................ 189
CHAPTER NINE .............................................................. 205
CHAPTER TEN ................................................................ 223
ABOUT THE AUTHOR .................................................. 247

# BOOK ONE

# CHAPTER ONE

*November 2012*

*The kiss deepened, his tongue teasing hers with just the right amount of pressure. His hands traveled lightly up her arms to her hair, causing her to shiver. She reached up to touch his face and neck; reveling in the feel of his warm, smooth skin. His hands moved back down, stopping at her breasts, caressing them gently. When he stopped abruptly, her eyes fluttered open and stared at him questioningly. Meeting her gaze, he slowly stood, took her hand and led her into a nearby bedroom...*

"You're conflicted about something."

The sound of Diana's voice jolted Ella back to the present. She was lying on the massage table, eyes closed, enjoying the heat that radiated from Diana's hands. She felt the energy stirring at the base of her throat, and then come to a halt. Blocked.

"Ella? What's going on with you?"

"Oh, nothing really. Just long hours at the clinic...." She forced a laugh. "I don't know what's more stressful, being a doctor or having two teenagers." The lie tasted bitter on her tongue. She had been going to Diana for months and had never lied to her before. Of course she had never told her the whole story either.

Diana paused for a moment, then inhaled and exhaled deeply. "You have a husband, Ella, and what about the boys? You are playing a dangerous game."

"What are you talking about?"

"You must get rid of him. This isn't good for you."

At the mention of *him*, Ella felt her body tense. How stupid she was to think that Diana wouldn't sense something! A Master Reiki healer and intuitive, Diana always sensed what was going on with her clients. She was usually right on the money, and this time was no different. For Ella indeed had a wonderful husband, John, and fourteen-year-old twins, Brent and Dirk. A year ago, she wouldn't have been able to imagine life without them, but now everything was different. Her passion for Milan was all consuming and overwhelming; it had a life all its own. That was the energy Diana was picking up on. Sure, she loved and respected John, and she adored her sons; yet she would give it all up for a life with Milan. It didn't even feel like a choice, just an undeniable fact.

"I don't—I mean, we haven't…" Ella took a deep breath. "He doesn't live around here…" She couldn't quite meet Diana's eyes; she was afraid of all she might see there.

"Oh, Ella, is this an online thing?"

"You don't understand," Ella replied, trying to control her voice. "This isn't just an affair … I think…"

She was about to blurt out the rest, but Diana placed

her hand on her arm. "Okay, okay. For now, just relax. You're supposed to leave here with less tension, not more." Then she brought the hand up to the space between Ella's eyebrows.

Ella closed her eyes again, feeling her Third Eye tingling. She knew Diana was trying to open it, so Ella would see the truth with greater clarity. The words she had almost said lingered on her tongue:

*I think he was my husband in a previous life and I have to find him.*

*February 2012*

For so long she had bought into the myth of her idyllic life. It wasn't *all* a façade, of course; she loved being a doctor, and her family had a beautiful home in Bellevue, Washington. Yet, at forty-one years old, Dr. Manuela Rowen—"Ella" to her friends, family and patients—remained unfulfilled. She realized that on some level she had simply been surviving, going through the motions of what was expected of her. Then, in one brief magical moment, everything changed.

She wasn't thinking of these things when she sat down in front of her computer that day; at least, not consciously. It was the end of an exceptionally long day at the clinic—two cases of MRSA, a six-year-old with strep, and a broken collarbone—followed by a marathon staff meeting. She had walked in, relieved to find the house empty. John, a chemical engineer, was working late on one project or another, and the boys were spending the night at a friend's. As always, her pleasure of being alone was accompanied by the slightest twinge of guilt; she took her roles as wife and mother very seriously, and she hated to shirk them, even in her mind. Still, she relished the sound of her footsteps echoing on the hardwood floors, and headed toward the study that doubled as her office. She took a seat behind the antique cherry wood desk, opened the laptop, and signed on.

She knew John thought she went a bit overboard in her monitoring of the boy's online activity; they were great kids who did well in school and had healthy face-to-face interactions with their peers, as well as on Facebook and Twitter. Still, they were only fourteen. She had seen enough teenagers in her practice to know that they led secrets lives—lives even the most diligent parents were completely unaware of. So she regularly went on the computer, checking the sites they had visited and sometimes drawing the line between what was appropriate and what wasn't. She had even begun to play some of the online computer games with them. It seemed like the best way to stay in touch with their interests and jargon, and to her surprise, she had found some of them to be quite addictive.

That night, as she perused through the search history, she came across a Roman civilization game. It was a role-playing game, designed to be played once or twice a day, for a few minutes each time. There were players from all parts of the world, which appealed to her. Ella created a character named "Venus" and soon found herself engaged in a slightly flirtatious conversation with another player named "Hero". No pictures or real names were used; the game was an anonymous outlet. Hero could have been a girl for all Ella knew, but it didn't matter because she wasn't trying to meet anyone.

Ella realized she could earn more "game money" if she had a second character, so she created "HealingGrace." She laughed softly at herself. Here she was, a grown woman playing computer games in her spare time. That was the best part, actually: relaxing, escaping, and playing like a kid. When she received a text from John that he would be at work for a few more hours, she laughed again, elated that she had more time.

HealingGrace made friends with a man in Australia named Theo76. They chatted about game objectives for a few minutes, then moved on to real life things like music, movies, and the other games they liked. After a short digital courtship, Theo76 proposed to HealingGrace for a game marriage, and she readily accepted.

After further acquainting herself with the game, Ella began looking for an opponent to fight. There was a player named "SINGUR" on the available fighter list, and she clicked on the name, trying to see if he or she had high enough stats to do a fight. SINGUR was a male character and had a game wife named Jasmine. On his public chat board, Jasmine had written, "I love you." On her page, he had posted a picture of a dozen red roses in a vase and a reply: "You are the most beautiful woman in the world. I will love you forever."

Ella felt embarrassed as she read these personal

messages between the two players, and immediately left without saying a word to him. But a few minutes later, SINGUR appeared on her chat board with a cryptic: "Hello." He must have seen her name appear and followed her.

As soon as Ella saw his name and simple greeting on her page, she felt the oddest electrical tingling; it began in her fingers on the mouse and traveled up her arm, all the way to her head. Within seconds, the strange electrical sensation had spread through her entire body. "*What the—?*"

She typed "Hello" back, then paused for a moment, still feeling a bit out of sorts. Then, on impulse, she quickly typed out a private message to him: "I'm so embarrassed. I didn't mean to read your private messages with your wife—I only stopped by to see if you could do a fight. Please forgive my intrusion."

He wrote back: "It is not a problem. It is nice to make your acquaintance."

Ella should have felt better, but somehow she felt even more off-balance. In fact, she felt a little lightheaded. She closed her eyes and took a few deep breaths, but the feeling lasted a few minutes. Thinking she was getting sick, she signed off the computer and went back into the kitchen to fix herself a cup of tea.

The next morning, Ella rose early, even though she didn't have to be at the clinic until the afternoon. She reached over and grabbed her cell phone from the nightstand to check her messages. She smiled at the text from John, an apology for working so much. He had come in after she was asleep the night before, and he had gone in early this morning. "I'll be home earlier tonight, I promise."

She sent him back a smiley face, then placed the phone back on the table and stretched before heading to the bathroom. As she brushed her teeth, she thought about the game she had played the night, and the strange reaction to SINGUR's message. She realized she felt a strong desire to chat with him again. *How strange! We didn't even really have a conversation—just my violation of his privacy.*

Strange or not, the feeling wouldn't go away, and a few minutes later, she was back in front of the computer, this time with a steaming cup of coffee. She signed into the game as HealingGrace and checked to see if SINGUR was online. He wasn't, so she spent a few minutes checking him out. He was from Romania and, based on his level and skill points, a fairly experienced player. Other than that, she couldn't really tell anything else about him. *So what made him so different?*

She looked at Jasmine's page next; it didn't say where she lived. She remembered the romantic words she had seen yesterday, and wished she had someone who spoke to her that way. She knew John loved her, but he had never been what one would call a romantic. Ella spent a few moments debating with herself, her fingers hovering over the keys, then she typed him a private message: "Why do you call yourself ... SINGUR?" and clicked "send". *He probably won't even reply.*

A few minutes later she was answering an email from a friend when she heard the telltale sound of a private message on the game website.

"It means 'alone' in the Romanian language. I spend a great deal of time by myself, but I am not lonely. Do you understand what I mean?"

There it was again! The strange tingling feeling in her hands, her arms, and then every inch of her.

"Yes, I understand. Just like one can be surrounded by people all the time, yet feel extremely lonely." *Like I feel most of the time*, she added silently.

She wanted to talk to him some more, but she didn't really have anything to say. Then she remembered a video she had come across on YouTube—a parody song called "Ooh, Girl – An Honest R&B Song" by Mike Polk. The gist of the song was that nobody can make love all night long. It had made her laugh out loud, and she had sent it to a few of her girlfriends. What could be the harm in sending it to him?

Still, she didn't want to make Jasmine jealous, so she sent him a private message: "I came across something really funny that I'm sharing with my friends. It has sexual innuendos in it. Would you be offended by something like that?"

She waited a few minutes, and when he didn't reply, she figured she had her answer. She hadn't gotten the impression that he would mind something risqué, but maybe he felt uncomfortable because of Jasmine. Oh, well. Shrugging off a twinge of disappointment, she logged off and went back upstairs to get ready for work.

When she signed on the next day, she told herself it was just to play the game. But there was no denying the uptick of her heart when she saw that he had responded to her message.

"No problem with that. ☺ Go ahead."

Ella paused for a moment, realizing that she didn't even know how old he was; then again, she was pretty sure, based on what she had seen already, that he wasn't a child. She sent him the link to the video, hoping he didn't think it stupid. Two minutes later, she felt that strange thrill when he sent back a string of laughter emoticons.

The next few days went by without a message from SINGUR, but Ella was too busy to notice. She was covering for one of the other doctors at the clinic, and the long hours and endless stream of patients hadn't left her a moment to sign onto the game. On the third morning, she woke up refreshed from a full eight hours of sleep, poured herself a cup of coffee, and headed for her office. SINGUR had sent her a message the night before, and smiling, she clicked to open it.

"It was a pleasure meeting you, HealingGrace. I want you to know that I am done with the game. I will be deleting my character soon."

A slight but unmistakable feeling of panic set in. Other players had come and gone and it didn't matter at all to her, yet this man was different, and she had absolutely no clue why.

"Oh no! I was just starting to know you! I wish you weren't going!"

As she pressed send, she realized that SINGUR was online. He wrote back immediately.

"I have to. I'm going on my own adventure, traveling to different cities across Europe for my work, and I won't be able to get online every day. I'm going to be gone about two months."

"You don't have to delete. You could just pause it," Ella typed, thinking quickly, "I just want you to know that I am a physician and an amateur psychic, and I KNOW you will return."

*Holy shit! Now why would I write that?* She never mentioned that she was "sensitive," not even to John. He was skeptical about such things, and it wasn't something that would go over well with the medical community. Only her best friend Shelby knew about her intuitive feelings and dreams. Ella knew she was trying to intrigue SINGUR, just as he had inexplicably intrigued her. He couldn't leave just yet, not until she could learn more about him.

SINGUR didn't remark on her revelation, though; he just sent a smiley face, Internet-speak for everything from genuine affection to patronizing good humor.

A few days later, she noticed that instead of deleting himself, he had paused his character as she suggested. That was promising, but, "amateur psychic" or not, she didn't really know if he would ever return.

February 29, 2012

Ten days later, she was doing one of her regular checks of the boys' online activity when she decided to sign on to the game. She told herself that she just felt like playing; she was not looking for a message from SINGUR. He had made it clear that he wouldn't be back for a while, if ever, and besides, it had just been a little casual chitchat. When she saw that he had left her a message, she realized she had been fooling herself.

"I'm out in the harbor diving for pearls," he had written, "hoping to find a giant black pearl worthy to give to you."

She didn't even question the tingling this time as she wrote the words "happy dance" on her page.

The next message she received from him was a link to the song, "Dance Me to the End of Love" by Leonard Cohen.

Ella had never heard of Leonard Cohen before, but she liked the song and his voice very much. It was deep, sexy, and romantic. She wondered if SINGUR was possibly in his fifties or sixties. Of course, it didn't really matter how old he was; she was married and lived a half a world away. Yet she couldn't deny that this man—this *stranger*—made her feel giddy. Was it something about him, or was she that desperate for a diversion? She didn't know, but she needed to find out.

*March 2012*

The next time she heard from SINGUR, he was in Amsterdam. He worked with computers, he told her, and was currently installing a system for a school. She told him a bit about her work, then asked him his age and whether he was married.

"Thirty-two and single," he wrote, "and what about you, HealingGrace?" She told him she was married, had two sons, and would be forty-two in a few weeks.

"Amsterdam, huh? Will you be heading to the Red Light District while you're there?"

"I went and drank coffee," he replied. "I saw the city at night and came straight to you." He attached a little blushing face emoticon to the message.

Feeling the heat rising in her own face, Ella decided to change the subject. She asked SINGUR how he managed to be online at the same time as her, given the time difference. Amsterdam was nine hours ahead of Seattle.

"I am awake during your daytime because I only require one hour per day of sleep."

He then told her that in addition to Romanian, he was fluent in English, French, Spanish, German, Italian, and Norwegian. Sleeping an hour a night left him lots of time to learn new things.

Ella was impressed … and more than a little envious. She couldn't function if she didn't have at least eight hours of sleep; her internship had nearly killed her. Imagine all the things she could accomplish, learn, and do if she didn't spend so much time sleeping! She would have time to exercise (be thinner), learn other languages (be smarter), and that was just the beginning!

*March 10, 2012*

*He guided her over to the bed, and had her lie down, face up, with her head on the pillow. Then he leaned over, kissing* her gently on the cheeks and forehead before bringing his lips to her own. He stroked her hair, and then stood up, still looking at her as he slowly took off his jacket and unbuttoned his shirt. Ella's body was tingling all over as she took in his dark hair, piercing green eyes and muscular chest.

Fully aware of his effect on her, he smiled rakishly and removed his pants, then returned to the side of the bed. Ella just lay there, trembling, waiting to see what he would do. He knelt near the bed and tenderly picked up her hand, kissing the fingertips. His lips traveled to her wrist, then up the entire length of her arm. He did the same with the other arm, and then moved to the foot of the bed.

Her eyes closed, Ella moaned softly as he crawled up her left leg, slowly removing the black silk stocking. He kissed the instep of her foot, then slowly moved back up the leg, smiling as she squirmed with pleasure. He moved to the right leg, removing the other stocking and tossing it on the floor. His kisses stopped at her panties, which he tugged at with his teeth but left in place.

He crawled over the length of her body, drawing up to her face. He gently brushed the hair from her eyes and looked deeply into them. As he kissed her, Ella could feel his hands unfastening her bra. She could feel every part of his body pressing against hers, then the delicious friction as he slid down again to kiss her breasts. He moved downward over her belly, then he was on his knees, straddling her. Slowly, he inched down her panties and flung them onto the floor, along with the bra and stockings; then let his gaze wander over her naked body as if he was worshipping something holy.

Ella reached out to caress his face, but he was already moving back down to her leg. He kissed the length of it again, but this time he used his tongue on her clitoris as his hands roamed over the rest of her. Ella climaxed, and then lay there in a foggy, euphoric haze. He crawled all the way up her body, showing her his hard cock.

As she caught sight of his erection, Ella gasped, thinking, "Oh my God. That is huge! That is going to hurt." But when she met his eyes, she relaxed and slowly took him in her mouth. He stayed there a few moments, then moved back to once again cover her with his body. She brought her eyes up to meet his piercing gaze as he slowly entered her.

He took hold of her hands, intertwining her fingers with his own, and pinned them down on either side of her head. They looked deeply into each other's eyes as he moved slowly and rhythmically in and out in a slow, beautiful dance. After a long while, Ella climaxed again; only then did he let himself go. Smiling contentedly, she fell asleep with her cheek on his chest.

Ella awoke feeling happier and more relaxed than she had in years. She stretched, and then quickly turned to look at the other side of the bed, as if she might find him gone. But there he was, his chiseled face even more beautiful in sleep, the long lashes of his eyes resting against his smooth skin. Ella resisted the urge to caress his face; she didn't want to disturb him.

There was a bathroom adjacent to the bedroom, and when Ella entered, she saw that he had put out some clean white towels and a fluffy white robe for her. When had he done this? She took a long, hot shower, then dried off and put on the robe. When she found her way to the kitchen, he was already there, drinking a hot cup of black coffee. Smiling, he nodded toward the pot, and poured her a cup. Ella sipped slowly as she surveyed the kitchen. It was beautiful, but seemed empty somehow, as if no one really lived there. Then her gaze came to rest on him, and he offered a crooked, tender smile. It was as if each was summing the other up and was pleased with what they saw.

With a start, Ella sat up straight in bed. Panting slightly, she brought a shaking hand to her forehead and wiped the beads of sweat away. It was early, the sun was just coming up, and John was sound asleep next to her. It was a Saturday morning like any other, except Ella had just awoken from the most vivid wonderful romantic dream. Yet it was not like other dreams; it was more like a movie, and she had been participating in it, not just watching. The only thing that made her doubt the experience was John's presence. So, it had to be a dream, right? Well, dream or not, she was floating in a cloud of euphoria that felt very, very real.

She took a few deep breaths, trying to re-acclimate to her surroundings; it was as if she was returning to her body after a long trip. Then, gingerly, she crept from the bed and went into the kitchen. She brewed a pot of coffee, poured herself a large cup, and headed to the computer. But she did not write SINGUR; she couldn't, not without knowing more about what had happened to her. Two hours later, when she heard John and the boys beginning to stir, she sighed and shut down the computer. She had read countless pages about astral travel and out-of-body-experiences, but she was still no closer to finding answers about her "dream."

All Saturday and Sunday, Ella walked around in a daze. Try as she might, she could not wrap her brain around this. Just as she knew that her body had been lying next to her husband, she knew that some part of her was thousands of miles away, begin caressed by SINGUR. She could still feel his touch, could even remember the smell of his skin—and the impact was crossing over into her real life. And it wasn't just that he happened to be drop dead gorgeous and ten years younger. He was also intelligent, cultured, and he made her feel like the most beautiful woman in the world.

By Monday morning, she couldn't stand it anymore. The only way she was going to get any answers was to talk about it with the one other person who had been there with her. She sat in front of the computer for a full ten minutes, growing more and more frustrated as she agonized over what to write. Finally, she signed onto the game, saw that he was online, and began typing.

"OMG! I just had an erotic dream, and you were in it with me, I think."

He replied immediately. "Oh really? Tell me about it."

"Well, to begin with, I wasn't married to John in real life anymore, and you weren't married to Jasmine either ... I mean, in the game.

"LOL, you call that an erotic dream?"

"No, I'm just trying to give you the background. Bare with me—I have a lot of details swimming around in my head."

"OK. :)"

Ella took a deep breath. "Well, we had gone out for the evening. I was wearing a slinky black dress, and you were wearing a sports jacket. You were bringing me home, to your home, I think. We entered the house, and went into the living room. I didn't recognize the living room, but it was nicely furnished. We were sitting next to each other on the couch, talking, facing each other. We each held a glass of wine that we sipped as we talked, and we laughed a little.

Ella paused in her typing for a moment, considering how to phrase the next part, then brought her fingers back to the keys. "Then your expression went serious and your face came close to mine. You have a handsome face, chiseled, like an actor. As we talked, you moved closer, slowly, all the while looking into my eyes, until all I could think about was you kissing me. When you finally did, I closed my eyes, savoring this first contact with you; the soft touch of your lips. My heart was pounding.

"Then you stood and led me to your bedroom. For a long time, we just kissed, but more passionately, with our hands roaming over each other's bodies. Your lips moved to my neck, and then I felt you unzip the back of my dress. You let the dress fall to the floor, until I was standing there in a black lacy bra, panties and thigh-high black silk stockings."

Ella paused again, wondering how explicit she should be. She decided that if she hoped to find out how real this connection was, she had to be honest with him. Taking a deep breath, she recounted the rest of the "dream," ending with their morning coffee in the kitchen. "And that's when I woke up. What do you think?"

Ella sat back in her chair and exhaled. She realized she had been holding her breath as she typed. A few minutes passed with no reply from SINGUR, and she half expected him to sign off, never to return. She had just closed her eyes when she heard the telltale sound of a private message.

"I don't understand."

Ella's stomach dropped. She didn't know what sort of response she'd expected, but she was fairly certain this wasn't it. She supposed she had been hoping he felt the dream too. She had put herself out there, and now he thought she was a stalker. While that wasn't the case, of course, she was embarrassed. Clearly, she had been subconsciously yearning for a night like the one they had shared, and now she had revealed her desperation to him. She heard the message sound again, reminding her that he was waiting for an answer. She glanced back at the screen.

"How did you know that? That is exactly the way I make love to a woman."

Ella gasped. "What?" she typed, her hands shaking. "Are you serious?'

"I am quite serious. I do other things too, LOL, but that tends to be my standard way. How do you know this?

"I told you—it was my dream, but it was more real than any other dream I've had ... Tell me, SINGUR, do you have brown hair and green eyes?"

"I have short black hair and blue eyes. Is that bad?"

Ella laughed. "No ... that sounds great. :)"

"Most Romanians have brownish black eyes, but in my family we all have blue eyes."

*Definitely not bad,* Ella thought, smiling.

March 11, 2012

"There is something that I can't figure out," SINGUR wrote the next day. "What kind of perfume do you wear?"

"I don't wear any perfume," Ella wrote back, both puzzled and excited by the question. "Some of the patients at the clinic have asthma and allergies, so we don't wear it. Why do you ask?"

Ella took a sip of coffee, nearly spitting it out when she saw his reply.

"I keep smelling this scent, something I've never smelled before, and I have this odd feeling it is you."

Ella was torn between elation and confusion. She was thrilled that he seemed to believe what she had written about the dream, and even dared to believe that he might be "smelling" her. But what did this all mean? Not knowing what else to write, she asked, "Do you wear cologne?"

"I wear Armani when I'm going out."

Ella tucked the detail away, then decided to table the subject for now. She steered the conversation to his work, and he told her he was still traveling, installing IT systems for Microsoft, Apple and Intel. His next stop: London.

They chatted for a few more minutes about the pros and cons of so much travel, and then she asked another question that had been on her mind.

"SINGUR, do you believe in God?"

As soon as she wrote it she began chiding herself. She

never asked anyone this question—she'd been raised to believe that making polite conversation meant avoiding politics and religion. But SINGUR wasn't just anyone—not anymore—and besides, these were some of the things that mattered most in life, not to mention the afterlife. If everyone obeyed this rule of polite talk, conversations would begin and end with medical issues and vacations; surely the American Revolution and countless other historical events would never have taken place. SINGUR may think she was a nut for asking, but Ella couldn't help but feel that God had something to do with this experience they were having.

"Yes, I believe in God."

Ella sighed with relief. She hadn't realized how much the answer mattered to her until she received it. She looked at the screen and saw he was still typing.

"I thought of something else I can tell you about myself. I travel with a watch collection."

"Hmm," Ella wrote back, relived that this time he was the one to change the subject. "That would suggest you have a love of fashion. You are quite the man, intelligent, hardworking, sexy, and stylish."

She paused for a moment, and then wrote, "So, why don't you like London?"

"How do you know I don't like London?"

"I don't know. It was just something I felt, as I read that you were going there."

A few moments passed before he replied, "I lost something very precious to me there."

"I keep hearing this song," Ella wrote, "and when I do,

it resonates in my heart and instantly makes me think of you—even though I don't understand why. It is by Greg Laswell, and it is called, "The One I Love."

SINGUR replied, "Thank you. I have one for you as well. It's called 'In My Secret Life' by Leonard Cohen."

She listened to his song several times, paying close attention to the lyrics. A vision started coming into her mind—a street near a hospital, late at night. There was a dark-haired young woman behind the wheel of a compact car. Then another car ran through a red light and hit her car on the driver's side at high speed. Both cars were completely wrecked. The young woman died on impact. The next thing she saw was SINGUR; he was wearing a long black coat, standing alone at the side of a casket. It was icy cold outside; there was frost on the grass near the gravesite. A funeral service was going on. They were talking about him, and the woman, and how terribly sad it was.

"OMG, I am so sorry. You loved a woman, and she died in London … I am so sorry."

"You are very perceptive, HealingGrace. I lost my fiancée in London in a car accident. She was killed by a drunk driver. Her name was Ioana. We dated for many years, and I loved her deeply. I asked her to marry me, but she was going to school to become a doctor, a surgeon, and wanted to wait until after she'd completed her residency. She was doing her residency in London. It happened one night as she was driving home after her shift. I had everything I wanted in life, until that drunk driver took it all away from me. That was almost a year ago. My heart turned to ice after that.

"I have a friend—a woman friend. She would like to be more serious I think, but she knows I don't feel that way about her. She is also my attorney. We work together. She asked me to play this game. LOL. I guess that is what makes you a good doctor, HealingGrace. You keep asking the questions until you get the answers you need."

Ella felt her stomach tightening. Her sadness for him was mixed with another emotion—it was something like fear. She knew it shouldn't matter that he had loved someone else, and probably still did. After all, she was the one who was married.

"Thank you for sharing that with me. I don't know how anyone can get over that kind of loss. I am very sorry. I wish I could send you a "hug" sign on the game, but they don't have one of those."

"Oh, is that what I get now ... just a hug? :)"

"I don't know, LOL, I guess we'll have to wait and see."

That night, Ella had a "dream" again, just as real and just as erotic as the first. She still didn't know what this was; all she knew is that she didn't want it to end.

*March 12, 2012*

"When I was getting dressed this morning," she wrote him the next day, "I figured out what I smell like. :) I use

Honey Almond body butter after I shower each morning. So, essentially, I smell like a large Chinese almond cookie!"

"That is it!" SINGUR replied. "I smelled it when I woke up. Did you come around again?"

She told him she had, and gave him some of the details. "Are you in London now?"

"Yes, baby. I'm in London, and I could say I'm home (one of them) ... but I don't feel like that."

"I have been thinking about this...," she wrote. "You are staying in an apartment that you shared with your fiancée, but then she died. I think it's time for you to give that apartment up and try to move on with your life."

"I think you are right ... no, I KNOW that you're right. It's finally time to clean out all my stuff. It was a strange day for me ... and I still try to figure out what is going on. It's something much more than ... I don't even know your name, but I feel you so deep inside me, in my soul, in my mind in my thoughts, my dreams, my passion, my desire. No, is not easy ... but if my life is complicated ... it is just because I can handle it. Many kisses ... with all my love. Because although I don't know how this is possible, I think I DO love you. M <3"

*March 13, 2012*

The next morning, Ella was so impatient to write him that she didn't even stop to make coffee. Hell, she was anxious to go back and reread his last message! Had he really said he loved her? She knew he had, but she couldn't resist looking at the words again.

"I felt something strange last night," she wrote a few minutes later, when she had managed to get a grip on her emotions. "I woke up with a start at 3 a.m., and I could feel this ... I don't know—frustration—about something. I didn't know what it was about. Then I went back to sleep."

"That was 11:00 a.m. here. I was sitting in my chair, waiting for the real estate agent to return my call. I was very frustrated. She was making me wait for hours. That is so bizarre that you could feel that."

Ella ran a shaking hand across her forehead. Her whole life she had been able to sense the emotions of those close to her—parents, friends, John and the boys. But sensing the frustration of a man she had never met? Bizarre didn't even begin to cover it.

March 14, 2012

On Wednesday morning, Ella awoke with her heart pounding heavily from another lucid dream. She couldn't wait to tell SINGUR.

"Oh my goodness, I had the most wonderful dream last night!! Do you want to hear about it?"

"Good morning, mon amour. Please tell me about your dream. :)"

She smiled, loving how he adapted to her time. With the eight-hour time difference, 8 a.m. for Ella's time was 4 p.m. for SINGUR, yet he wished her a good morning, as if he were with her.

"Well, it was raining very hard outside. I was in an apartment, sitting in a big brown leather armchair near a window. Behind me, I could hear the water dripping off the roof and water rushing down the sides of the street. You were working at a laptop computer on the couch, which was against the wall. The couch was made of fabric with a pattern in earth tones.

I decided I would take a bath, and give you some space. I went to the bathroom connected to the master bedroom and lit some vanilla candles, placing them around the tub. I turned on the hot water and while the tub was filling I went to the kitchen to make myself a cup of vanilla coffee. Then I returned to the bathroom and added some vanilla bath bubbles to the water. I was naked, except for a white towel wrapped around at the bust line. I had my long dark brown hair pinned up to keep it out of the way. I turned on some soft instrumental music and bent over to test the water temperature.

I stood when I felt your soft approach behind me. You wrapped your arms around my waist and nuzzled my neck with kisses. You turned me towards you, and pressed your lips to mine, your tongue delicately teasing mine. I pulled your tee shirt over your head, and returned your kisses, urging you to continue.

There was a scent of vanilla in the air. You gently pulled my towel off me, growling with desire and approval. Then you picked me up in your arms and took me, not to the master bedroom, but the other bedroom in the apartment.

It was decorated in tans and browns, and had a chocolate-brown dresser with a large mirror. There was a queen size bed. I could see the whole room so clearly, and the smell of vanilla was tantalizing. You laid me horizontally on the bed, face up, with my neck at the edge so my head was slightly dangling off the bed.

You walked up to where my head was and unzipped your pants. I saw how ready you already were. You put your cock into my mouth and did a slow in and out motion. I closed my eyes. I could smell your skin. You stopped and took your clothes completely off, then moved around the other side of the bed and crawled on top of me.

You kissed my lips, then rolled me onto my stomach and kissed my back. It was very sensual, and I was getting very turned on. You reached underneath me and found my breasts, pinching them ever so softly as you bit and kissed my neck. When you entered me, I let out a moan of pure pleasure.

We made love there slowly, for a very long time ... then again, and again. The way you move your body, and the way you stop before you lose all control and reposition us ... it was amazing. I felt everything as if it was truly happening, even though in reality I was back in my own bed, completely motionless. It felt like our intercourse lasted for hours off and on. Mmmm ... I'm still floating on a cloud, just remembering."

"How do you do that?" he wrote. "It is like you can see everything that is around me! And vanilla is my favorite scent."

Ella giggled, typing, "And I was just wondering to

myself how *you* did it...." She smiled sadly.

"I don't know how it works, I just know I like it. But I am troubled. I want you to know that I would never cheat on my husband. I love him, I married him, and I would never cheat. I'm not that kind of person. But now I have all these feelings for you, which I love too. *No one has ever made me feel the way you do.* It is like I'm filled with this amazing heavenly bliss."

In reply, SINGUR sent her a link to the song, "Kiss the Rain" by Billie Myers.

"Thank you, SINGUR. Good night."
"Good night, my beautiful lady."

# CHAPTER TWO

Ella wasn't sure when she started thinking about her relationship with SINGUR in a spiritual way. At first, it was just something delicious, something that was hers alone. It did not belong to her husband, her kids, or her patients; it didn't even belong to SINGUR, despite his starring role. And while she certainly considered the "dreams" curious, she had simply allowed herself to get caught up in the exquisite pleasure.

Once she had considered sleep to be a "necessary waste of time," something she needed to keep her mind and body functioning. Now she slipped into bed each night, as excited as a kid on Christmas Eve, a delicious tension building in the pit of her stomach, for she knew she would soon "be" with him again. And those once dutiful trips to the computer to check emails or the boys' activity had now become her time to share those dreams with SINGUR and find out what he was doing, thinking and feeling. It all felt so innocent, an escape that did not touch her real life. After all, it wasn't like she had picked up some guy at Starbucks! Her interactions with SINGUR were carefully compartmentalized, and probably temporary, she reasoned. One night the dreams would end, or he wouldn't answer a message, and that would be that.

But the dreams didn't end, and he always answered her messages, usually with yet another surprising and delightful detail about his life. She found herself thinking about him during the day, when she was seeing patients, talking with a friend, or making dinner. Then came the day when she realized that her "life" with SINGUR was as real as the one she shared with John and the boys.

"Mom. *Mom?* Mom!"

Ella looked up to find Dirk looking at her with that mixture of amusement and disdain particular to teenagers. He had been trying, unsuccessfully, to get her attention, and she had been reliving her night with SINGUR. They had been in his home again, and it was becoming more familiar to her.

"I'm sorry, honey, what were you saying?"

"I *wanted* to tell you about my school project...."

"Okay, I'm here," Ella said, hiding her guilt behind a smile.

Dirk was removing a thick stack of papers from his backpack when his phone started ringing. He glanced at the caller id and grinned. "Sorry, Mom, gotta take this, be back in a minute."

This time Ella's smile was genuine—she knew very well what "a minute" meant. But as soon as Dirk left the room, her thoughts quickly returned to SINGUR and what he truly represented in her life. Her dreamlike experiences had begun slipping into her home life, her life with her children, and this worried her. She wished she could put her finger on how they made her feel ... euphoric, no doubt, and somehow familiar.

The clarity, sudden and undeniable, forced Ella to sit straight in her chair. This feeling she had when she was with SINGUR was familiar because it was how she had felt one night, long, long ago; it was a night she didn't often revisit because of the agony it caused. It was night of the accident that critically injured her and killed her first love.

1983

They were an unlikely couple. She was a straight-A student, shy bordering on introverted, with long brown hair, brown eyes, and a broad smile that made her "cute" rather than "hot." Jason was her opposite—a popular, handsome football player, known more for touchdowns than his GPA. They probably never would have met if not for that student driving course sophomore year, although Ella liked to believe that they were fated to cross paths.

The driving class had already started when Jason walked in—tall, blond and beautiful. Within two minutes he had charmed the instructor—a stickler about punctuality—into letting him stay. Ella watched as he scanned the room for an empty seat, then grabbed the one next to her.

As the instructor continued his lecture, she made notes in the margin of the Rules of the Road pamphlet. A few times, she felt as though the beautiful boy next to her was staring in her direction, but she did not raise her head. She was a confident girl—her mother had instilled that in her—but she had no illusions. Guys like that did not notice girls like her. They went to parties and dated girls with big hair, tiny clothes, and flirtatious grins.

A few minutes later, the teacher announced that it was time for the practical. He took the group of teenagers outside to the lot, where several cars bearing "Student Driver" signs were parked. He told them to each get into a car, start the engines, and wait for his instructions; they were going to practice driving in a circle, very slowly, one behind the other.

When it was her turn, Ella approached her car and got in. Just as she was climbing in, she heard arguing from the vehicle behind her. The blond guy was leaning into the driver's side window, an angry look on his handsome face. Another boy, already seated behind the wheel, looked equally annoyed, but finally got out of the car, grunting, "Uh, sure, Jason, whatever you say," then "What a jerk!" once he was safely out of reach.

Ella watched the exchange, then slipped behind the wheel of her own car. When she glanced in the rear view mirror, she saw that he was grinning again. *What is he up to?*

The exercise commenced, and for the first few minutes they practiced driving and stopping. There was even a pretend traffic light. Ella's sweaty palms slid over the steering wheel, and she wondered again what the blond boy had been up to. She hoped he wasn't planning on bumping into her car for kicks. The school would probably charge her parents for the repairs, to say nothing of the embarrassment. She kept an eye on him in the rear view mirror, and whenever he saw her, he waved and smiled.

When the class ended, Ella's mother was already there to get her. She had started walking towards her mom's car when she heard someone call out, "Wait!" Ella glanced behind her to see the blond boy jogging smoothly toward her. "Hi, I'm Jason."

She offered him a shy smile. "Uh, hello. I'm Ella."

"I was wondering if I could have your phone number," he said, his eyes steady on hers. Ella could barely hide her surprise. She had never received much attention from the boys at school; in fact, she had never had a boyfriend, or a date to a dance, or even a first kiss. She couldn't believe this gorgeous boy—and an athlete by the look of him—would show an interest in her.

Her face growing hot, she told him she didn't have a piece of paper. "Good thing I do," he smiled, handing it to her, along with a pen. She wrote down her name and number, handed it back to him, then practically ran to her mother's car. After she had closed the door, her mom said, "He seems like a nice boy. Who is he?"

Ella's cheeks flushed even redder as she replied, "He said his name is Jason."

Ella spent the next twenty-four hours trying to convince herself not to get her hopes up, and had nearly succeeded when she heard the phone ring. A moment later, her mother called out, "Ella, the phone is for you."

Ella picked it up, "Hello?"

"Hi Ella, this is Jason, from the driving class ... do you remember me?"

"Yes—yes," she stammered, "Of course I do."

Jason laughed, easing her nervousness, then asked her

where she went to school. That began a conversation that flowed seamlessly, without even a touch of teenage angst or awkwardness. It was as if they had known each other for years and were simply catching up on life's little details. She learned that Jason went to O'Dea High School and played for the football team. Also a sophomore, he was a few months older than Ella; in fact, he was turning sixteen the very next day and heading directly to the DMV to get his license. The driver's class had been his last.

Below she knew it, two hours had passed. As they were about to hang up, Jason said, "Would you like…?"

He paused, and Ella thought, *this is it, he's going to ask me out.*

"…to come to my birthday party on Saturday? It's just a small family thing at my grandparents' house."

Ella gulped. *Grandparents' house?* She couldn't believe she was going on a first date—ever—with a gorgeous, popular guy *and* meeting his family at the same time. Ella knew she should be flattered, but all she could feel was the butterflies in her stomach.

"It's nothing fancy," Jason continued, waiting for her reply. Was it her imagination, or was he nervous too?

"Yes," she said finally, "I would love to."

"Great!" he said, then told her that he and his parents would pick her up around 4:30.

Still in a daze, Ella said goodnight to Jason and slowly replaced the phone on the receiver. She lay on her bed, smiling to herself for about a minute. Then, she sat up in bed with a gasp. What was she going to wear? Luckily, she had plenty of outfits conservative enough to meet someone's grandparents. After a few days of sifting through every inch of her closet, she decided on a sundress with a light sweater.

On Saturday afternoon, promptly at 4:30, Ella was checking her hair one last time when she heard a car pull up. She went to the window to see a sea foam-green Mustang sitting in her driveway. Jason, looking even more handsome than she remembered, climbed out and walked to the front door.

Ella hurried downstairs before her parents could do any damage. She walked into the foyer as her mother Virginia offered him a friendly hello, and her father, Richard, shook Jason's hand and sternly told him to have her home by nine.

She kissed her parents goodbye and followed Jason out to the car. He held the door open for her, then joined her in the backseat. As they drove to his grandparents' house, she kept stealing looks at him—the wavy blonde hair, the gorgeous medium-blue eyes, the muscles any girl would die to touch. Luckily, his parents kept her distracted with questions about everything from her school to her family to when she planned on getting her driver's license.

Finally, they turned onto a lovely, tree-lined street with modest brick homes. Ella was wondering which one belonged to his grandparents when she heard Jason exclaim, "Wow!"

In the driveway was a pickup truck—red, with a white stripe; a ribbon of a darker shade of red was wrapped around the hood. Jason didn't wait for the Mustang to come to a complete stop before leaping out to inspect his birthday present. Ella smiled as she watched him running his hand lovingly along the hood, then she shyly trailed him and his parents into the house.

Jason hugged everyone, thanking them for the birthday wishes and the truck. Then he introduced Ella to them as if *she* were the guest of honor. Like Jason, his family immediately made her feel welcome.

After a simple but delicious meal of barbeque ribs, corn on the cob, coleslaw and salad, Jason's mother and grandmother began clearing the table so they could make room for the cake. Ella was about to help them when she felt Jason's hand on her arm.

"Come with me," he said, then clasped her hand and headed outside. A moment later, they stood on the porch, his hand still holding hers and his gaze steady. "I really like you," he said quietly, "a lot."

Then he moved his face closer to hers. Ella closed her eyes and felt his hand touch her face, then his lips gently pressing against hers. It was a fleeting, magical moment, yet it felt like an eternity. They would have stayed there longer if Jason's younger brother Tim hadn't come looking for him so they could sing happy birthday and cut the cake. Soon after, it was time to get Ella back home, which Jason proudly did in his new truck.

From that day on, they were inseparable, talking on the phone every night and seeing each other every weekend. He took her to dances at his school and the after-parties with his friends. Ella's parents were a bit concerned about how serious she and Jason were getting, especially after Ella asked to transfer to O'Dea. In the end, though, Richard and Virginia couldn't deny that Jason was a wonderful boy and seemed to worship their daughter, and they gave their consent.

Ella was nervous before starting O'Dea, but she had no reason to be; she was dating one of the best football players on the team. His friends became her friends, but despite her instant popularity, Ella never lost sight of her goals. She continued to get straight A's; she just made room for fun too. She and Jason graduated high school together, and applied and were accepted to the University of Washington. Although Ella was excited about starting college, what mattered most to her was being with Jason. Every moment she spent with him had this surreal quality to it; he had literally transformed her life.

FALL, 1986

The music was playing loudly as Jason's truck sped along the winding, mountainside road. It was a Friday, and they were headed to dinner at their favorite Italian restaurant. Ella fiddled with the radio, then brought her hand to rest on Jason's leg. He shot her a knowing grin as she ran her fingers lightly up and down his thigh; he always teased her that she got frisky when in the truck, ever since that warm summer night at the drive-in when she had lost her virginity in the back cargo bed. That had been the summer before college, and now, here they were, sophomores at the University of Washington. Jason was studying to be an educator, and while Ella's major was still undeclared, she was gravitating toward the sciences. She couldn't believe how fast the time had flown, or how her stomach still tightened whenever she saw or spoke to him.

There was something in the air that night; the autumn air was crisp and cool, and the leaves were shades of green, yellow, red, and orange. It felt like something was about to happen.

"Jason, what do you think about getting an apartment—living together?" she said softly into his ear. She felt his face stretch into a smile.

She was waiting for him to verbalize his answer, when she felt his thigh stiffen under her hand. There was a shape standing in the road directly in front of them, eyes toward them. The proverbial deer in the headlights.

"Oh my God!" she yelled, putting her hand on the dashboard, getting ready for Jason to come to a quick stop.

"Shiitttt!" he screamed.

Everything that followed happened in slow motion. Jason, both hands on the wheel, trying to go around the deer. Swerving to the right. The truck going up an embankment, hitting the guardrail and bouncing to the other side of the road. It felt like they were sailing through the air, then—POW!—the truck connected head on with a tree.

Ella heard herself scream, but she didn't feel it; it was as if it came from outside herself. And it had, because she was now hovering over the vehicle. She watched as the deer darted away, unscathed, saw that the driver's side of the truck had been crushed as if it were tin foil. The truck was on its side, exposing its underbelly. She saw the first spark of the flames, and thought, *What about the people inside? Why aren't they moving?*

Suddenly she realized that she was watching Jason

and herself die in a tragic car accident. Amidst the flames licking the twisted steel, she saw a cloud of mist emerge, rise slowly near her, then continue upward to disappear into the evening sky. She knew at that moment she should be feeling a sense of surrender and peace; she didn't. Instead, she felt an unexpected, seemingly boundless rage. She looked up towards the sky and sent out a furious thought: *REALLY? Come on! I have to die in a fire AGAIN?*

Throughout her life, Ella had always been respectful when addressing God. She believed God to be loving and all-powerful, and that one should always address God with respect, gratitude, and humbleness. But she was feeling anything but humble at this moment. She felt betrayed.

So she was quite unprepared for the quick reply: *No, not this time. This time you will live. You can get out and LIVE.*

She had heard the answer, yet it didn't seem possible, for she was still out of her body. Time once again slowed to a crawl, then stopped altogether, and a gradual peacefulness and euphoria came over her. Just as she was beginning to think, *okay, I remember this joy ... I could stay this way forever...,* time restarted and—bam—she was back in her body, broken, burned and in excruciating pain.

People had arrived on the scene and were screaming outside the truck door, asking her if she could move. She couldn't, though, for she was held in place by the seat belt; neither could she communicate verbally. She saw the flashing lights of a police car, the shriek of an ambulance. She heard steel twisting as they removed the door, then the people pulled her out of the truck. Two paramedics put her on a gurney and carefully loaded her into the back of the ambulance, climbed in and shut the doors. She could smell the scent of burnt skin and hair emanating from her, could feel the unimaginable pain that was still nothing compared to the heartbreak. She knew Jason was dead.

The ambulance tore away from the scene. Someone was leaning over her, staring at her in puzzlement. "What are you saying, Miss?" Ella realized her lips were moving and that she had been reciting the Lord's Prayer over and over and over.

The next week was a blur of sleep and worried-looking faces, all underscored by a horrific pain. Her parents were there and of course the hospital staff, but they brought her little comfort. There was only one face she really wanted to see, but she knew, with an altogether different kind of agony, that it was not possible. Then, on the seventh night, Ella opened her eyes to find a strange white mist gathering at the side of her bed. The mist materialized into a transparent image of Jason. He was dressed as he had been the night of the accident. He gave her that tender grin she so loved, then he began to speak. It took a moment for Ella to realize that although his lips were moving, she was hearing the words inside her head.

"*Ella, I love you,*" he said, his beautiful voice filling her brain. "*I want you to know that I am in a good place, and that I am happy. I want you to get better, and find your own happiness. I will always watch over you, and always love you.*"

Ella tried to sit up, and when that proved impossible, tried to reply. The only sound that emerged was an unintelligible croak through her cracked lips.

Jason grinned. "*Still stubborn, I see. Just rest, Ella, rest and get well.*" Then he leaned over, kissed her lovingly on the cheek, and disappeared. She shook her head back and forth, eyes wide open. Yes, she was awake, and Jason's spirit had just visited her room.

She decided not to tell anyone about what she had seen. She feared her parents would worry that she had brain damage, and the nurses or doctors … well, they just might decide she was getting too much morphine and cut her dose back.

The next day, she learned that she would be in the hospital for at least another month, followed by another year of physical therapy so she could learn how to move her body again. Ella held it together until the doctor left, then broke out in low, painful sobs. More hospitalization meant more time to think and reflect, and that meant thinking about Jason and all the things that would never be.

A week later, another strange event occurred. It was late at night, and Ella had been given her last dose of painkiller. And it was in that half-awake, half-sleeping state that her thoughts wandered to what she would do when she was well—what she should do with the rest of her life. She had already been blessed in so many ways: she had always been healthy, and pretty—or at least she had been until she was burned. She had wonderful parents who were still clearly in love with each other and doted on her and her sister, Penelope. Both girls had been adopted as infants, yet were as close as any blood relations. Their home was full of love, and then she had met Jason and was blessed all over again.

Now he was dead, and she had been spared. Surely, there had to be a reason.

But what? Her mother had always told her that everyone had gifts, but what were hers? She smiled as she thought about her knack for knowing the name and medical use for every type of plant. She didn't even know where she had picked up that knowledge; it just seemed to be part of some mental blueprint.

She might have been dreaming, but she wasn't sure. She didn't see anything, but she heard in her mind a man's voice say, *"You shall be a doctor and a mother. It is very important that you hear me and understand me. In this lifetime, it is imperative that you have RESPECT. You are a healer, as before, but RESPECT is very important to you in this lifetime. In addition, it is important that you have children. You will be their mother and their teacher."*

Shortly after leaving the hospital, Ella became aware that something was different. Outwardly, things were getting back to normal; her wounds had begun to heal and, according to the medical staff, would barely be noticeable. If she continued to recover on schedule, she would soon be able to resume classes. But something had definitely changed. She kept having all sorts of dreams, and while they were certainly realistic, they were different than any other she'd had before. Unlike her other dreams, she was not really a part of them; it was more like she was watching them on a screen. Sometimes they made sense and other times they didn't. She'd figured they would go away as the concussion healed, but they did not.

Neither did her memories of the crash; not the happy

moments before they came upon the deer, not the moment that jolted her out of her body and above the blaze, and certainly not the moment when Jason materialized beside her hospital bed. For six months Ella tried to push them from her mind, for they always brought back the agony of losing him. Finally, she realized they would never stop haunting her until she got answers. A couple of years before, she had heard of a psychic named Rose; she had given readings to some girls in the dorm. They had referred to Rose as "spot on" and one girl had even handed her card to Ella, who promptly tucked it away in a textbook. She had always dismissed it as nonsense, but now she had nothing to lose. She found the text, packed away in the one of the boxes shipped to her parents' house after the accident, and sure enough, the card was still there. Ella called to make an appointment. In a kind, almost motherly voice, Rose took down her full name and the month and day of her birth, then penciled her in for the following week. Just before she hung up, Ella heard Rose chuckle and say something about how she loved to read skeptics. How had she known?

Ella told no one about her appointment; on the day of it, she told her parents she was meeting a friend for coffee and drove out to the address Rose had given her on the phone. The door was answered by a short, stout woman with bright blue eyes and short auburn hair. "Come in, Ella, come," she said warmly, and led her to small, comfortable kitchen. There was a round table covered with a floral tablecloth, and she gestured for Ella to take a seat. Ella noticed a box of tissues had been placed in the center.

Rose sat down across from her, closed her eyes, and

took a deep breath. A moment later, she opened her eyes, and they were even brighter than before. For the next hour, she shocked Ella with knowledge of Ella's past, including the accident and how she had lost someone very special. She even described Jason's appearance and sense of humor. But what shocked Ella most was that Rose validated her strange experiences—how she had left her body the night of the accident and how Jason had visited her in spirit—she even knew about the mysterious voice that had told her she would be a healer and a mother. Ella's eyes began to well, and Rose handed her the box of tissues. "You will go into medicine," she said, "and have two children."

By the end of the appointment, Ella felt both drained and peaceful. She thanked Rose profusely and stood to go. "You're welcome, dear," Rose replied, as she walked her to the front door, "And you're always welcome to come back, although Lord knows you don't need to." Ella looked at her quizzically. "Well, you have the gift as well, never doubt it."

*Me, a psychic?* Ella didn't know if she believed that, though Rose had indeed turned out to be "spot on" about everything else. She decided to put it all out of her mind, take comfort in the fact that Jason was at peace, and concentrate on moving forward with her life. And that was what she did; she kept every physical therapy appointment and, when they gave her exercises to do at home, she did twice the recommended amount of reps. She also began catching up on her coursework, and a year after the accident had resumed a full course load.

One chilly January night, she walked into the library, looking for a spot to sit and study. The place was packed, and table after table was full. Then she walked by a young man, seated alone at a table for three. He had light brown hair and was wearing a green sweater.

Suddenly she heard a voice inside her head say, *"That is Him. He will be the father of your children."*

Ella's first instinct was to look around, for she hadn't heard that inner male voice in quite some time. But no one else seemed to have heard anything, and besides, it was more of a knowing, or a feeling, than a sound. It definitely felt like some other sort of entity was communicating to her, not an ordinary person.

Ella continued on, only to find herself back at the young man's table a few minutes later. "Would it be all right if I sat down here?" she asked, "this seems to be the only free seat."

"Sure, it's okay," he replied, throwing a quick glance her way before returning his own studies. Ella noticed that behind his wire rim glasses were intelligent hazel eyes.

"Thanks." Ella sat down, opened her binder and textbook, then pulled highlighters of various colors out of her bag.

Try as she might, though, she could not seem to focus on her work. Her mind kept returning to what the voice had said: *"That is him. He will be the father of your children."*

But she wasn't even thinking about dating, let alone marriage or kids! She was only twenty-one years old, and besides, she was completely focused on her goal of becoming a doctor. After forty-five minutes of reading the same paragraph, she sat back in her chair and sighed in frustration. The young man looked up, and their eyes met.

"Can't concentrate tonight, huh?" he asked. "Me neither."

And that had been that. His name was John, and he was friendly and easy to talk to. He enjoyed the outdoors and camping. He wanted to be a father someday. He enjoyed sports. He liked to golf. He liked watching a variety of sports on television, mostly football and basketball. He was gentle and a nice person. He was handsome in his own way. They never had the sort of fiery passion she and Jason shared, but they did have a love built on friendship and common goals. They married after three years of dating. On her wedding day, she couldn't help smiling to herself about how the voice had predicted it.

But without a doubt, Ella felt her intuition most strongly—and with the greatest degree of accuracy—during her internship. Her thoughts always ran to the night the Hispanic truck driver came into the ER. He was coughing and had trouble breathing. The resident listened to his chest, declared it was pneumonia, and ordered antibiotics. Ella, who was standing beside him, heard a voice say, "Coccidiomycosis!" Startled, she looked around, then realized that the voice had come from inside her head. "Coccidiomycosis," the voice repeated, "he needs intravenous antifungals or he will die."

When Ella suggested to the resident that they should consider the possibility of fungal pneumonia, he only mocked her. It was only after the man ended up in the ICU that he ordered the culture, which came back positive for Coccidio. Thankfully, the man got the therapy he needed in time to save his life.

Then there was the patient who complained of a sore throat after his surgery. All the other doctors were reassuring him that it was normal post-op, but the voice told Ella that his dentures were stuck in his throat. She looked at his denture holder, which was empty at his bedside, and asked him to smile. He showed his gums, and when she asked where his dentures were, he said he didn't know. Once again, she summoned the courage to speak up and say she thought his dentures were stuck in his throat. Once again, the others tried to make her feel as if she didn't know what she was talking about, and once again, she was proven right.

The strange moments of intuition didn't happen every day; in fact, they were quite random, and beyond her control. But what really threw her was when she and the resident went to pronounce patients dead. Ella would see that wisp of mist leaving the body, the one her resident never seemed to notice. This didn't make her psychic, though, or did it? More importantly, she had left her own body once, that night after the accident. Could it be that the same thing was happening when she visited SINGUR in her dreams?

Was it possible they weren't dreams at all?

# CHAPTER THREE

*March 15, 2012*

As Ella became more convinced that her experiences with SINGUR were indeed astral projections, she became obsessed with finding out more. But how? Perhaps a psychic could tell her, but she didn't know of one she trusted, and it wasn't like she could ask anyone she knew for a recommendation. *"Excuse me, Dr. So-and-So, you know any good mediums?"* They would laugh her out of the clinic! In the end, the scientist in her won out: she would conduct a "clinical experiment." She just needed some time when she wouldn't be disturbed by John or the boys.

The opportunity came the next night; John was working late again and the boys had a tennis lesson. As soon as they had left, she changed into loose-fitting yoga pants, then went to set up her meditation space. She had chosen her office; it was spacious yet cozy, and she felt very comfortable there. It was also the first place she had connected with SINGUR, albeit over a computer. First, she shut off the ringers on her landline and cell phone, then she went to gather her supplies. From the linen closet, she grabbed a soft towel; from the kitchen, a book of matches and a thin white candle. When she got to the closet, she spread the towel over the area rug near her desk. Then she lit the candle and placed it on a low table so that the flame would be eye level.

When the space was ready, she lowered herself to the floor and sat cross-legged on the towel. Then she took a few deep, slow breaths, focused her gaze softly on the burning candle, and tried to empty her mind of distractions. As usual, the first few moments were the most challenging. Ella did not fight the mind chatter though, as she had found this to be a fruitless exercise; instead, she waited patiently as the thoughts flitted through her brain: *Why are you wasting your time? This is not going to work, you know! Or, her favorite: You are absolutely insane.* She continued breathing deeply for a few minutes, until she finally felt herself relax. She then asked SINGUR for permission to examine him, and was surprised when she felt him agree. Not because she didn't expect to get his permission, but that she had sensed his response at all.

Suddenly she found herself in a brightly lit examining room furnished with only a steel table, like the sort they used at the clinic. SINGUR stood on the other side of the table from her, smiling quizzically. She asked him to disrobe and lay face-up on the exam table so she could do a head-to-toe skin exam. He threw her a sexy grin and complied. Ella slowly approached the table, taking in his beautiful form. *You're only here for an inspection,* she reminded herself.

He had short, thick black hair that was a little spiked on top. His skin was olive-toned and completely free of blemishes. His eyes were a deep blue color and punctuated by thick, dark eyebrows. He was clean shaven, except for narrow sideburns that reached nearly to his earlobes.

Ella was less surprised by his physique, for she had felt it so many times that it was almost as familiar as her own body. He wasn't skinny, but he didn't have an extra inch of flesh either. His neck was strong, and he had broad shoulders and a nicely defined chest with a smattering of dark hair. She noted the small, crooked scar under his chin, as well as a one-inch linear scar on the front of his left shoulder. His abdomen was beautifully chiseled, as were the muscles on his arms and legs. Like his face, the skin of his body was clear, with no acne, moles or warts. The biceps and triceps of his arms were nicely muscled, but not overly so. Scanning further downward, she thought *aha!* and laughed. There was a tiny bit of fungal infection on his left third toenail. He was almost perfect, but still human.

"*Roll over, please,*" she thought to him, and he followed her command. "Beautiful lats," she murmured, then allowed her gaze to sweep appreciatively over the V-shaped back, the muscular buttocks and legs. He certainly was a thirty-something hunk.

She mentally offered SINGUR her gratitude for allowing the examination, then she slowly came out of her trance. Her eyes fluttered a few times, then opened with a start. "Wow!" That had been incredible. Now to find out whether she just imagined it, or whether it was true. Still taking slow, deep breaths to acclimate back into her body, she got up from the floor, walked over to her desk, and sat down.

As soon as she signed on as "HealingGrace", she saw that SINGUR was online. Her heart skipping happily, she began to type.

HealingGrace: I just did a physical exam on you. You have a scar on your left shoulder, another on your chin, and a little fungus in your nail on the left foot. You have no moles or warts that I could see.

SINGUR: LOL, I felt you. You are right about everything except one thing. I have no scars on my body, only scars on my soul.

HealingGrace: Are you sure about that? I saw them so clearly.

Ella paused for a moment. During the exam, she'd had the fleeting thought that something might be wrong with a relative of his—possibly his mother or father. She debated about whether she should ask; what if it was upsetting and he didn't want to talk about it? Finally, though, she just decided to come out with it.

HealingGrace: I was just wondering, how are your parents doing?

SINGUR: That is strange that you would ask me that!

I just found out my mother is ill and I need to go see her right away. She is in hospital, and my father is very worried.

HealingGrace: Oh, I'm very sorry to hear that! I'll say some prayers for her to get well soon.

SINGUR: Thank you, baby. Now I'm sorry, but I need to get a little rest before my flight.

And with that, he was gone. That night, Ella dreamed she was on a plane, resting her head on his shoulder, her body relaxed and her eyelids heavy. She felt a little nudge, and heard him say, "We're landing now. It's time to wake up." Ella woke up abruptly, looked around, and saw that she was in her bed; John was sound asleep beside her. She immediately looked at the clock and saw that it was 11:50 p.m. That was strange, she thought to herself, but she went back to sleep.

*March 16, 2012*

The next day, Ella signed on to find out whether SINGUR had made it safely to Romania. She was disappointed, but not surprised, that he wasn't online. She sent him a quick note asking about his mother, then went about her day. She tried to keep her mind on whatever she was doing, but SINGUR plagued her thoughts even more than usual. That night, she was elated when she signed on again and saw that he had responded.

SINGUR: Yes, baby, I got to Bucharest this morning and went straight to the hospital. My mother has kidney disease, and it is pretty advanced. She is to begin dialysis immediately. Thank you for asking.

Ella was about to reply when she saw that he was still typing.

SINGUR: I must tell you, something very bizarre happened during my flight ... I could see and feel you on the plane with me. You were sleeping with your head on my shoulder. When the plane landed I told you it was time to go, and then we gathered our things and got off the plane together.

Ella gasped, her heart racing. She took a few deep breaths, waiting for it to slow to its regular thud-thud. This was incredible.

HealingGrace: I felt that, too!

SINGUR: It seems like you are always with me, sometimes I talk out loud to you, like a complete fool.

HealingGrace: I know what you mean, because I'm feeling it, too. It is like wherever I go, there you are. I wish I knew what was happening between us.

SINGUR: I wish the same, baby. Maybe one day we'll find out.

Then, pleading exhaustion, he signed off. Ella felt a hard bite of loneliness and reminded herself that she would see him in her dreams. "Maybe one day...," she said, echoing SINGUR's message. But "one day" wasn't good enough. Not anymore. She signed out of the game and brought up the Google home page. It was time for a little research.

An hour later, Ella had ordered several books online. One of them, *When Two Souls Connect, The Real Soul Mate Story*, by Steve Gunn, arrived two days later. Ella waited until John had fallen asleep, then glanced guiltily over at him before pulling it out of her nightstand. From the first page she was hooked, and read straight through to the end. When she finished, she glanced at the clock, shocked to see that it was 4 a.m.! She was about to put the book back in her nightstand, shut the lamp and go to sleep when she realized that she wasn't the least bit tired. Careful not to wake her husband, she slipped out of bed and headed down to her office.

As she signed onto the computer, then the game's website, she felt like an anxious schoolgirl. Was she about to say too much? Would this scare him off? Finally, she decided that it was better to find out now before it went any further. She wrote him a quick explanation of the book, then she flipped to the page she had dog-eared, and began typing the list for him.

HealingGrace:
How to Recognize a Soul Mate
- You met under unusual circumstances
- Feels like you've known them forever
- "S/he isn't my usual type, but there's just something about him/her."
- You don't need to speak to communicate
- Looking into their eyes, you see deep into their soul
- Your soul mate is on your mind 24/7 and you can't change that
- You sense your soul mate and know what they're thinking and feeling.
- Your interests change to more spiritual things
- Desperate to be with them and contact them all the time
- Feel totally at peace when you are with them
- Feel like a teenager again
- You know that somehow you have changed and there's no going back

In many soul mate cases, one or both of the partners will be:
- Already in a relationship with some level of commitment, but not emotionally satisfying
- Be scared of commitment
- Have been badly hurt in the past
- Suffered emotional problems
- Is still or has recently been in a controlling relationship
- Have moved from relationship to relationship, moving on when they are required to commit

- Most always, one of the partners will be sufficiently spiritually developed to understand the significance of this relationship and that it is a life-changing event. And almost always one of the partners will be "sensible" and try to "do the right thing" on a very practical level.

Physical symptoms of soul mate connection:
- You feel like a different person, more alive
- A tugging feeling in the heart
- Headache behind the eyes
- Stomach churns and flutters
- Sleep patterns and diet will change
- Feeling "lovesick"
- Sometimes, when you're apart, you feel a panic like you have lost someone close
- An overwhelming feeling that life is not worth living without the soul mate or, conversely, a new awareness that life must be worth holding onto if such feelings of love are possible.

Ella clicked send, a lingering feeling of doubt flitting through her mind. She glanced at the clock. It was now 4:20 a.m. She thought about John, asleep upstairs, with no idea that his wife was communicating with another man—a stranger—on the computer. *I should go to bed,* she thought. But she didn't move. Any guilt she felt was not enough to make her give up SINGUR, or her quest to find out what they really meant to each other.

HealingGrace: I know this is a lot to lay on you right now, especially with all that's going on with your mom. But as soon as I read this book, I knew I had to tell you ... because what it says, that is exactly how I am feeling! I love how I feel when I am with you, like I am totally at peace. It is wonderful! And there is more, SIGUR, something I would never tell anyone ... maybe I didn't even realize it myself. Before I met you, *I was tired of living.* It wasn't as if I was going to commit suicide, I would never do that. But I was having these talks with God, asking, *"Is this it, then? I've done what you asked. Now what should I do?"* But I never got an answer back; and I was so unhappy. I'm married, and I love him, and I know he loves me, but I wasn't feeling loved, or appreciated. It had even gotten to the point where I was avoiding him, and I think it is because he has become so controlling about everything, and he says things sometimes that really hurt my feelings.

Ella paused again, shocked by what she had just written. She had never allowed herself to consider John controlling, because that would mean that she—a strong woman—was allowing herself to be controlled, at least to some extent. But now, as she wrote SINGUR, all her feelings were bubbling to the surface. How John never seemed pleased by her, and hadn't in a long time, and how the house always had to run according to the way he liked things. Ella was about to sign off, when she heard the telltale noise, signifying that SINGUR was now online. She immediately typed, "How is your mom doing?" so he wouldn't think she was only concerned with herself.

SINGUR: The doctors say she will get out of the hospital in a few days and be fine, but will have to likely continue with dialysis until she can find a transplant.... Now I see that you have sent me messages, so give me a minute to read them. :)

She waited nervously for him to read them, thanking God that he didn't know her name, in case he decided she was some kind of stalker. After what seemed like an eternity, she saw that he had replied.

SINGUR: I'm so sorry to hear that you've been unhappy. All I can say is that I am here now, and that you have saved me too.

Ella nearly burst into tears of relief.

HealingGrace: Okay, since you feel that way, there is more, LOL. Here is what Steve Gunn says about Soul Twins:
"Meeting the soul twin, sometimes referred to as 'twin flame', is quite a rare experience. As we are all on a different part of our path and have different abilities to feel and understand love, how can we possibly know that our current relationship is as good as it gets? Soul mate relationships teach us, harden us, open us and help us grow spiritually until, if we are very lucky, we will be ready for the ultimate, the twin soul relationship.
"The only connection that time never dulls, and we never quite get over, is the soul twin.

It takes a soul on a relatively high level to fully feel, sense and understand the connection in a soul mate relationship and to be freely able to wholeheartedly abandon themselves to it. Hence soul mate connections happen to old souls.

So, if you're in one, it's a sure bet that you're an old and spiritually developed soul and you have already visited this earth in many previous forms, each time returning on a higher level as your lifetimes have been tasked with learning your karmic lessons."

SINGUR: I don't really understand this. But, people have called me an old soul. I never knew what that meant.

HealingGrace: People say that to me too, that I have an old soul.

SINGUR: I am very confused, because it's like how the books describes—how I feel about you. I think about you all the time.

It was near dawn when Ella finally crawled into bed. She knew she was going to be tired all day, but it was well worth hearing that SINGUR felt the same as she did. Yawning, she pulled the covers up over her and closed her eyes. Suddenly, she felt a hand touch the side of her face and run through her hair. A second later, a pair of full lips gently kissed her forehead. Completely startled, she looked around to be sure John wasn't playing some sort of trick on her. But he hadn't stirred at all. She would swear on a stack of Bibles that she had just been kissed good night, and that someone had just stroked her hair. Her last thought before she fell asleep was that she must be losing her mind.

*March 17, 2012*

HealingGrace: Last night I had the weirdest experience. It felt like someone touched me, and when I looked around, no one was there. Yet, I felt calm and peaceful.

SINGUR: LOL, that was me. I kissed your forehead and touched the side of your head, whispering to you, "Good night and sweet dreams," like I usually do…. sometimes I just want to look at you, watching how you drink your coffee, brushing your hair or simple things, then I want to kiss your lips, kiss your neck, touch your hand, to look in your eyes and tell you how wonderful you are.

Ella stared at the computer in shock. *Like he usually did?* She wondered whether their conversation about soul mates had somehow deepened their connection, allowing her to feel his touch. At that moment, she wished she could call Steven Gunn and ask him.

HealingGrace: Really? But how do you know what time I go to bed?

SINGUR: I learned your schedule very quickly when

we first met. Don't you know how bad I want you? I want nothing more than to be your lover. I'll kiss you and hold you ever so tight … I will never forsake you or leave you behind.

HealingGrace: OMG, this is tearing me apart. I don't know what to do or think anymore.

SINGUR: Did you feel anything else…?

Ella was about to write that she hadn't, but then she remembered the dream—if that was even what it was—two nights before. They had been together in a bedroom on the first floor of a house—his house, but not the apartment she had visited before. They were on the bed, kissing and touching, then he reached into a drawer in the nightstand and pulled out some black ties and a blindfold. He asked if she was interested in trying them out, and she nodded, a smile upon her lips. Then she lay back on the bed, giving herself over to him. He slowly undressed her down to her bra and underwear, then gently tied her wrists to the headboard posts so that she was lying comfortably with her arms outstretched. He then tied the blindfold around her head. It was tight enough to block her view, but not tight enough to hurt her. Now she was relying completely on touch and sound, and found it was a turn on. She had always been curious about this kind of thing, but had always been too embarrassed to ask John for it. But with SINGUR, she didn't have to ask; as always, he just seemed to know what she wanted. As he made love to her, Ella quickly lost herself to the sensual feelings, and came faster than she ever had before. He held off, though. After making love to her with her on her back, he untied the wrist ties, left the blind fold on, and turned her over onto her stomach. This time, he did climax, then he removed her blindfold, and looked into her eyes with an angelic smile on his full lips.

Ella wrote him back, telling him about the blindfold and black ties. He responded immediately, bolding his words for emphasis.

SINGUR: **Yes, that is right. I think this is all quite simple ... I am your dream man, and you are my dream woman.**

HealingGrace: I think you are right.

HealingGrace: Oh, by the way, March 21st is my birthday.

SINGUR: Amour, I know about your birthday already. I hope you have a wonderful celebration. My next stop is Geneva. I'll be traveling while you sleep.

HealingGrace: OK, good night. Sweet dreams.

Ella signed off, unable to keep the grin from her face. *But how can he know about my birthday when he doesn't even know my name?* It seemed as impossible as everything else that was happening, and yet, there it was. What's more, Ella found that in that moment, she didn't really care how he knew; she was just thrilled that he did.

*March 18, 2012*

The next day, though, Ella found that she *did* care about SINGUR's public chat messages to his game wife, Jasmine. Her stomach clenching, she read the romantic things he said to her, saw the pictures of roses he still sent. Had SINGUR just been playing her all along? Any man *that* good-looking was probably with lots of women, and she just really wasn't into that sort of man. That was why she had married John, because he was dependable, reliable, and faithful; he would never cheat on her. European men that looked like this man should only be dealt with using a ten-foot pole, in her opinion. Damn it, though, why did she have to be so attracted to him?

SINGUR: You really think that about me? I'm not like that.

HealingGrace: What?

SINGUR: I do not have sex with many women. I am not that way.

HealingGrace: You heard me thinking?

SINGUR: Yes.

Ella shivered, and ran her hands along her arms to get rid of the goose bumps. *How does he do that?* She was thinking about him too much, all the time, to be precise. She was married, and despite John's flaws, she did love him. She also adored her children. Nothing good that could come of this—whatever it was—with SINGUR. She wracked her brains, trying to come up with "deal-breakers" that would leave her no choice but to end it. For one, she couldn't stand being around smokers, and she knew a lot of Europeans smoked. Also, she preferred tall men, and she didn't think she would consider being with a man shorter than her. For the life of her, though, she couldn't remember how tall he was in the "examination" she given him.

HealingGrace: So, tell me. Do you smoke? How tall are you?

SINGUR: I don't smoke. I am as tall as a skyscraper. :)

HealingGrace: There must be something wrong with you. What are your vices? I might as well know now, just in case it's something I cannot live with.

SINGUR: Hmm ... let's see ... I'm an alcoholic, I sleep with prostitutes, and I kick dogs in the street, LOL.

SINGUR: Seriously ... no, I do not smoke. I drink a little wine when I have dinner with a beautiful woman, but not every day. I don't go near prostitutes or kick dogs.

My biggest problems people would say are that I drink too much coffee and I'm a workaholic.

Ella was thinking that didn't seem so bad. People would say she was a workaholic too; in fact, it often seemed like all she had was her work and children. She felt a sudden flare-up of jealousy towards Jasmine, then she felt stupid for feeling that way because her relationship with SINGUR was just an illusion and couldn't go anywhere.

Illusion or not, it was incredibly hot. She thought back to the night before, when they had ripped each other's clothes off in a frenzy. Then he'd picked her up, placed her on the kitchen counter and fucked her like a crazy animal, hard and fast. She loved it. She felt like a raging porn star. She had to laugh at herself in the morning. Her dream life was so different from her real life.

Her mind was dazzled, amused, and confused. It really seemed like this man could read her thoughts; not only did he know how she was feeling, but he was also acting out her most secret sexual fantasies. What was going on? She couldn't deny that she was having a great time, but she didn't want to get hurt.

The beep of the computer startled her from her thoughts.

SINGUR: It seems like it must be your turn.

HealingGrace: What? Oh. Are you saying what I think you are saying? Is my psychic lover telling me that I'm not holding up my end of our affair?

SINGUR: Yes.

HealingGrace: OK, fine then. It seems like I've been a better receiver and you have been a better sender. I have sent things to you but you haven't seemed to receive them. Fine, we'll do a little experiment then. I'll go sit down and think of something, and then you write back to me what it was. OK?

SINGUR: OK :)

Ella went to her bedroom, closed the door behind her, and lay down on the bed. She calmed her mind, gradually finding that point of steady breathing with no extraneous thoughts entering her head. Then she began to create, imagine, fantasizing. She wanted to come up with something so unique that even if he got just a little bit of it, even if he said one key word, she would know he got it. She created an elaborate scene, and was quite pleased with herself when it was done.

A few minutes later, she got out of bed and went back to the computer.

HealingGrace: Well? Did you get that?

SINGUR: No, I didn't feel anything. Tell me.

HealingGrace: LOL, OK then. I was really hoping you would receive it on your end.

Let's see. :) It is a clear evening and we are in Rome. We have a plan to visit the Coliseum together, but at night, when no one is there. We are good planners, you and I, so we gather everything we will need for the evening.

We have some small wood and kindling to build a fire, a couple of warm blankets and pillows, music ... and costumes. We plan to change once we get there. We have costumes that look like our characters in the game. You have an ancient warrior costume with the metallic chest plate and red sleeves, and those high, lace-up sandals that leave your knees showing. My costume is a pale green gown that ties on one shoulder, leaving the other shoulder bare. And it is sheer, so you can see my golden bra and matching panties underneath. A golden belt ties around my hips, and I have a wreath of small flowers to wear in my hair.

I will be your maiden servant, and my job is to make you comfortable and provide you with any pleasure you desire. We have a spread of food that includes grapes, cheeses, bread, wine, water and assorted meats. Since we have so many things to bring, we decide to use a small wheelbarrow that we see nearby. That way, as we cart all of our stuff down the cobblestone path approaching the Coliseum, we won't strain our backs.

Once we arrive, we explore a little bit. We go down to the bottom level, where the narrow passages are, and we play a little hide and seek, like children. I'm giggling and having a wonderful time. Then we choose a place for our role-play. There is a little grassy area off to one end. It is on the level above the small passages, where the main bottom level would have been. There are marble ruins all around us. It is dark now, and no one is around. While I go to find a secret place to change my clothes into the Roman maiden outfit, you lay out the blanket and build our fire. When I return, you go off to change into your costume. While you are gone, I start some soft music playing on a boom box I brought along and lay out the food.

When you return, looking incredibly strong and sexy in your garb, I ask you if you would like to lie down and make yourself comfortable on the blanket. You do, leaning back against the pillows. The fire provides just enough warmth to keep us comfortable in our scant outfits. I tend to the fire as needed, and offer you food. I feed you nibbles of bread and grapes with my fingers, and I offer you a golden goblet filled with wine when you are thirsty.

You say you would like me to dance for you, so I do. Seductively, I gyrate in front of you, turning slowly to the music, so you can see my front and backsides. You ask me to remove my belt, and I do. I toss it by your feet. You ask me to remove my filmy dress, and I do. I use it as a sash and lean in towards you, teasing you with my breasts. Then you kiss me, and I wrap my arms around you.

Breaking off the kiss, you ask me to dance some more, then to remove the rest of my clothing. Blushing ever so slightly, I do as you ask, grateful that there doesn't seem to be anyone else around. I approach you now, completely naked, and kneel at your side. We begin kissing. I can feel your hands exploring every part of my naked body. Then your mouth moves down, and you are kissing my shoulders and my breasts. I surrender to my passion for you. You lift up your soldier's garb, exposing to me the fact that you have no underwear on, and I can see that you are quite taken with me. Using only the expression in your eyes, you let me know you want me to take you into my mouth. I use my tongue and my lips, and you get harder and harder and harder. Then you stop me, before it is too late.

You guide me upwards so that you are lying back and now I am straddling your head. My pink velvet slit is directly over your mouth now, and you proceed to give me exquisite pleasure with your tongue, while I run my fingers through your hair. I can feel your hands running over my butt and thighs. I feel as if I'm a cat, purring with delight, and the pleasure builds until it becomes almost intolerable, and I cry out with my orgasm.

Everything gets somewhat blurry at that point, but then I realize you have positioned me so that I am all fours, on my knees and arms, so that my back is a table. You are still fully in your costume. You come behind me and enter me, and as you do your hands are touching my breast, and stroking my clitoris again. You go at me sort of hard and fast, but it doesn't hurt. It only feels so breathtakingly good. I hear you make a final grunting noise then, just as you come into me. Sweating with exertion, we both collapse onto the blanket. You hold me in your arms, and we spend the rest of the evening, sipping wine in front of the fire. It is pure bliss.

As Ella finished typing, she realized that her face was hot and her palms were sweaty. Still, she giggled when she saw his reply.

SINGUR: Wow. I just love the Coliseum, LOL. I wish I had felt it. I'd like to do that for real.

HealingGrace: Yeah, so would I. So would I.

*March 19, 2012*

When Ella awoke from the next dream, her heart was going a mile a minute and she was damp with sweat. Like the ones before it, this encounter seemed to be even more detailed than the last, both of SINGUR's person and his surroundings. All five of her senses had been engaged, or was it all six?

HealingGrace: Wow, I had a crazy night.

SINGUR: Another one, LOL? What happened?

HealingGrace: This time, it was a beautiful sunny day and we were out looking for an apartment. The real estate agent brought us to one, then left us alone so we could take some time to consider it. We were happy, and feeling rather amorous. I was wearing a white halter dress like the one Marilyn Monroe wore. You were in jeans and a gray sweater.
  The front door of the apartment opened into a living room. On one side of the living room was a large glass

door. On the other side was the kitchen. We were looking at the apartment, smiling, and then we looked at each other. I pulled my iPhone from my purse and put on some music. You took me in your arms, and we waltzed around the apartment. You are a great dancer. You knew how to lead well. We danced like we could compete in a dance competition, we were so good. It was easy to dance because the rooms were large and empty of furniture. I felt so happy. You brought me closer and kissed me.

I felt a wicked surge run through my body, a powerful desire for you. We kissed again, more deeply this time. You are a rascal. You unloosened the knot on my halter dress and let the top fall down from my waist so my breasts were exposed. You began to kiss them, and I stood there with my head thrown back, letting myself savor the sensation of your mouth on my skin. I was getting very aroused. I pushed your back against the divider wall between the kitchen and the living room. I unzipped your pants, got down on my knees in front of you, and took your cock in my mouth. You got very hard. You were breathing heavily. You stopped me before you came. You pulled me up by my arms, and kissed me on the lips some more. The kitchen floor was linoleum, and the living room had this short tan carpet. I still had my dress on though the top part was down. You had me sit down on the carpet where you took off my shoes. My stockings and bikini underwear came off next. You removed your sweater, but left your pants on. There was no furniture so we were trying to figure out what would be most comfortable. You rolled our sweaters into a makeshift pillow, which you placed on the floor against the living room wall.

You leaned back and I sat on top of you. We kissed some more, and your hands were everywhere, getting me more and more excited. Then you guided yourself into me. I moaned with pleasure, and we rocked together in and out, until we both climaxed. We lay there on our backs for a few moments, just smiling at each other. That's when we heard the real estate agent's shoes approaching the front door. We got up quickly, laughing and dressing as fast as we could. That was when I woke up.

SINGUR: You are so amazing! Yes, my love, we are in Geneva. I was looking at an apartment with a realtor who did leave me alone in the place for a while. I was thinking of you.

HealingGrace: You are an incredibly sexy man. :) I liked the apartment, by the way.

SINGUR: You are the most amazing and beautiful woman in the whole world. I liked the apartment also.

*March 20, 2012*

HealingGrace: I've been trying to guess your real name, and all I "hear" is that it begins with a T.

SINGUR: My name begins with M, LOL.

HealingGrace: So does mine! My name is Manuela Rowen, but most people call me Ella.

Ella stopped, mentally chiding herself for giving him her real name—and her full name, at that!

SINGUR: My name is Milan. It is nice to meet you. :)

"Milan." Ella said the name aloud, trying the feel of it out on her lips. Oh, the absurdity of this. They had already shared such intimacy, yet were only now learning each other's names! She still didn't know his last name, but for now she would be happy with what she had.

The bigger problem was that she was clearly in love with a man she didn't know except in her dreams, and she knew she would never meet him. No matter what she did to try to stay busy, her mind kept going back to him and the sensations he created within her mind. She couldn't figure out how her brain was being stimulated in this way, by a stranger who lived on the other side of the world.

HealingGrace: I wonder why I kept hearing a T. Oh, I know … I think it stands for Trouble. :)

SINGUR: Trouble, I could be that, too. :)

HealingGrace: Milan, I have a confession to make. I'm afraid that I have fallen in love with you. I never intended for this to happen. Do you understand? I love my husband, but I am not "in love" with him. I have fallen in love with you ... and I have no idea what to do.

SINGUR: Now I'm sitting here, just staring into space like a fool. I keep telling myself this can't be true, it can't happen to me.

Ella felt the beads of sweat gathering on her upper lip. As hard as it was to ask the question, she knew she had to or she would go crazy.

HealingGrace: Do you love me, Milan?

SINGUR: Yes, I love you! This is just my frustration! I give you all my love, my passion ... and I don't know why! You are in my life ... not just in this stupid game.
 I feel you everywhere I go, around me, you're with me ... and you are not even here.
 I feel you when I look around ... I'm tempted to ask you if you like it ... this place, this apartment, etc. ... and after all ... I am just alone ... I stand here and asking myself if I am crazy or what?

I was so happy yesterday ... feeling the need to dance, to make love with you here, to go out shopping. How does it seem—all these things—to you? I have a woman in my life ... but really SHE is NOT!

Yes, this makes me crazy because I can't understand ... why you? I can have any woman I want ... and again ...

why you? Definitely, I am crazy!

HealingGrace: Well ... I can tell you that I am not so bad. I am fairly attractive, and intelligent. I have a good sense of humor and most people enjoy my company. I think I'm a pretty good catch, actually.

SINGUR: LOL, I have no doubt that you are all those things, mon amour. I love you, I really do.

# CHAPTER FOUR

*March 21, 2012*

SINGUR: Happy Birthday, baby.

When she saw the words, Ella's eyes welled with tears. That morning, John had barely managed to mumble happy birthday and give her a chaste peck on the cheek before running out the door. Yet somehow, a man she had never met in person made up for her disappointment. She read the next line of his message: "Did you get what I sent you?" and knew that something was waiting for her in that incredible, impossible, ethereal place in which they met.

HealingGrace: No … here, let me try now. It doesn't just "happen," you know. I have to calm my mind or be at the edge of sleep, either going down or waking up. Please, try to send it again now.

SINGUR: Okay.

She had felt lonesome before, but now she was grateful that no one else was home. She sat back in her chair and, staring at a fixed point on the wall, began taking slow, deep breaths. She held each breath for a count of four, then pursed her lips and slowly exhaled, expelling any preconceived notions of what she was about to receive. She did this a few times—letting the thoughts melt away, enjoying the feeling of relaxation that was spreading throughout her body like delicious nectar.

Suddenly, a scene materialized before her. She knew she was still sitting in the chair in her office, yet she also stood a few feet away, with Milan. They were in a rather generic hotel room, presumably somewhere in Geneva. It was like a transparent overlay, yet startlingly real.

Her mouth slack with surprise, she watched herself and Milan dressing to go out to dinner. She wore a strapless sequined, navy blue, floor-length gown, and her dark hair was swept off her neck in an artfully messy twist. He had on a tuxedo with a black tie. Smiling, he offered his arm; she slid her own through it, then he escorted her out of the room and into a wide, carpeted hallway.

Smiling, Ella closed her eyes and took another deep breath, as if to inhale the moment. When she opened them, she and Milan were seated at a table for two. They were outside now, on a deck with a view of the city lights. Despite the fact that it was March, the air was warm and fragrant.

The table was beautifully set, with long white candles burning brightly in the center. To Ella's right, a bottle of champagne sat chilling in a bucket of ice. The waiter came over and poured them each a glass. Raising his, Milan said, "To us, my love." She clinked her glass to his, then, gazing into each other's eyes, they took a sip. Ella held it in her mouth for a moment, letting the bubbles tickle her tongue. It was ice-cold, delicious, and very expensive. Milan had seen to every detail.

A few minutes later, a different waiter returned with a food-laden tray resting on his narrow shoulder. Ella did not remember ordering—they had not even seen a menu; yet somehow her favorite meal—lobster *fra diavolo*—had materialized in front of her. Milan had the swordfish, and they enjoyed every rich bite while listening to the soft sounds of a violinist playing a few tables away. She felt like a princess.

After their plates had been cleared, Milan reached into his pocket and handed her a small, velvet box. She opened it and saw a necklace—a large sapphire surrounded by diamonds. She stared, perplexed, as the necklace transformed into a ring, and then magically transformed itself into a bracelet before becoming a necklace again.

Her confusion turned to laughter as she realized she was witnessing the indecision in his mind; he was trying to figure out the right gift for this point in their relationship. He had settled on the necklace, which was lovely, but it felt good to know that a ring had been considered. Smiling broadly, she thanked him for the beautiful piece, and he stood, went behind her chair to fasten it. His fingers lingered on her slender neck, sending chills up her spine.

They returned to the hotel, but not to the room they had left. Instead, they were entering a grand suite, with at least thirty large vases of cream and pink roses carefully placed throughout the sitting room. There were cream and pink rose petals scattered on the bed. There were candelabras with lit candles. Wordlessly, Milan slipped her dress off and let it slide to the floor. Then he led her to the bed.

Usually, when she spent the night with Milan, she awoke to find him already gone. But now, in her birthday vision, she opened her eyes the following morning to find him lying beside her, looking down at her with a gentle smile on his lips. Ella was still grinning broadly as the vision faded from view. She felt as if she floated back to her computer.

HealingGrace: That was amazing. Thank you. :)

SINGUR: I told myself I would never do such a thing—that I would never be with a married woman. I never wanted this. But with you, I cannot help myself.

HealingGrace: But how can you know so much about me? So many details about my wants and needs—from my favorite meal, to the fact that I wanted to see you lying next to me in the morning?

Several agonizingly long minutes passed as Ella waited for Milan to answer. Had she asked too much of him? Had she dreamt the whole thing? A palpable weight settled around her shoulders, and just as it was creeping toward her heart, she heard the computer *ding* with his reply.

SINGUR: I want to tell you a story about myself. It's something I don't tell too many people, but ... with you ... well, I think it's time you know. I hope you won't think I am crazy...

Ella laughed out loud. He was worried that *she* would think *he* was weird?

SINGUR: ...but I think it might explain why I know these things about you. When I was twenty years old, I woke up one morning and had a premonition that I was going to die—that day, in a car wreck. I had a very fast car at the time. Even though I was young, I had already done many things with my life, and so I accepted my fate. My aunt asked me to drive her to the airport. I agreed, and my cousin came along for the ride. As we were leaving my house, I kissed my mother on her cheek, and said, "Goodbye, I love you. I think this is the last time you will see me alive." My mother laughed at me and said, "Milan, don't say such things!" Because you see, this is also me, always trying to make people laugh, so she thought I was making a joke. We go to the airport and drop my aunt off. I kiss her on the cheek goodbye. My cousin asks to drive my car back and I agreed, even though I knew he wasn't very experienced with handling sports cars.

Sure enough, he was speeding down the road and lost control of the car. It rolled and landed on the passenger side. My cousin was all right, but I had a collapsed lung. I smiled to myself because I knew this was coming, and I had accepted that this was how I was to die.

I was rushed to the hospital. On the way, I remember leaving my body and floating up into the clouds. Everything looked so beautiful, and I remember thinking I was happy to go, I was at peace. But then I was told that it wasn't my time yet and I was being sent back into my body. I woke up in the Intensive Care Unit with my girlfriend and my family at my bedside. I thought maybe I had dreamt the whole thing, but later on, I found out that the doctors had, at one point, pronounced me dead.

That was many years ago—today I am completely healthy. But in the shower this morning, I looked down at my chest, and you know what? I DO have a scar, where the chest tube was placed when I was in the ICU.

Anyway, I am telling you this because ever since that happened to me, I have been able to feel love in one's emotions. It can be very troubling at times. For example, if my mother is crying, I will feel it, and I'll know I have to call her. It works this way. I feel your emotions, too.

Stunned, Ella reread his message. Her thoughts flew back to her own accident, the sensation of floating out of her body and having a different mental vantage point. What were the chances that Milan had had a similar experience, and at nearly the same age? She hadn't even told him about her own accident, or what had happened to Jason. And, after several moments of consideration, she decided it was not yet the right time. Besides, she was still on cloud nine from her "birthday present" and she did not want to spoil the moment.

As if on cue, she heard the front door open. It was the

twins, who had come straight home from school to make her a special birthday dinner. They did it every year, and it was nice, even if John rarely made it home from work in time to join them.

"Happy Birthday, Mom!" she heard them shout in unison. She called out a loud thank you, then hurriedly typed a reply to Milan.

HealingGrace: All I can say for now is that I do not think you're crazy—I would never think that. In     fact, I understand you more than you know.

*March 22, 2012*

The next morning, Ella waited for John to leave for his run, then she hurried to the computer. She had barely slept, so preoccupied was she with the story of Milan's near-death experience.

HealingGrace: Thank you for telling me about your accident—now, you should know something about me. When I was nineteen years old, I was also in a car accident. I also nearly died and had an out of body experience. I was burned over much of my body, but I healed with virtually no scars. But even more important, I started noticing strange things—internal things—about myself that I've been unable to share with anyone—until now, with you.

I don't understand what is happening now, I really don't. But I do know that I can feel your emotions. It is taking some getting used to. I'll get little waves of sadness or lust sometimes, and I'll think, I wonder what triggered that? Then I'll think ... I bet that is Milan right now.

There is something else you need to know about my accident—my boyfriend Jason was killed. I loved him very much. The love I felt for him is different from the love I have for John, and different from the love I feel for you. The love and desire I feel for you is nearly overwhelming at times. It is like being consumed with a fire that is always burning just out of control.

I have thought a lot about you and me, trying to figure it out. Now I think our connection is even stronger because of the trauma we went through. I also think we're not just experiencing each other's emotions, we're *magnifying* them. When we're both happy, we feel extremely happy, and if we are both sad, then we feel the unbearable sadness. The only solution I can think of is to make sure that we are both happy all of the time. I love you. M <3

SINGUR: Thank you for sharing this with me.
For so long I have been trying to resist you, fighting with myself, telling myself this couldn't be happening, or that you were too good to be true. Then I began to realize that I was just scared, because our feelings are so strong. After that, I was willing to understand you, to love you unconditionally, to give you all my love and passion

without expecting anything in return.

I don't ask you anything because I don't need to. I can "feel" you. There is still a lot I don't understand, but it does not matter. All I know is that I am hopelessly, crazy in love with you.

They chatted for a few more minutes. Then, after telling her he was going on the road again for work, Milan signed off. Ella was so happy she nearly floated through the rest of her day. Even John noticed her unusually good mood, and when he asked her about it, she told him she had saved a very ill patient at the clinic. The lie rolled smoothly off her tongue, and while she knew she should have felt guilt about it, she didn't. After all, it was harmless, right?

Ella was still smiling the next morning when she headed downstairs and straight for the computer. These days, she didn't even stop to make coffee first because she was so excited to see what Milan had written during the night. But when she saw what he had written today, her heart froze in her chest.

SINGUR: Hi baby, how is your day? I'll try to stay away from you, give you some space. Baby, I think it is time for me to quit the game. There are many things that I need to take care of, and not much time there. All my love, M<3

Ella sat for several minutes, trying to fight the panic that was welling up inside her. What had changed since their last conversation? It didn't make any sense. Should she even reply to him? "Oh, fuck it," she muttered, and with angry, staccato motions tapped out a message.

HealingGrace: What?! Please don't leave the game, how will we talk?

She pressed send, then sat back and waited. Several minutes passed … and there was nothing. Ella didn't realize she was holding her breath until she heard the computer make its telltale sound. She was surprised and greatly disappointed when she saw the message was not from Milan, but another player from the game—someone named "Karmagirl".

Karmagirl: Are you feeling sad?

Ella snorted with annoyance. She was upset enough without getting some random, intrusive message from a stranger.

HealingGrace: I think you may have sent this to the wrong person.

Karmagirl: No, I meant to write you. So are you feeling sad?

HealingGrace: I have no idea who you are, but I really don't have time for this right now.

Karmagirl: I'm sorry—it's just that I sensed your

feelings. I have what you might call "a special gift" for that.

In spite of herself, Ella was intrigued. She quickly looked at Karmagirl's character page and saw that she had been on the game for several months. She was a member of a different clan and was "game married" to a character named MathewDark.

HealingGrace: That's great. Look, I'm sorry if I seem unfriendly, but I have a lot going on here.

Karmagirl: I know you do, that's why I'm writing you. I've had the gift all my life. My father also
has it, and he taught me how to use it.

Ella sighed. Should she confide in this stranger? She was certainly dying for answers about Milan's sudden change in attitude, but she didn't want to make some desperate mistake and give information to some online scammer. My God! If it ever got out she would be a laughingstock. She could see the headlines now: *Local Doctor Conned by Online "Psychic" Thieves.* Finally she decided she couldn't feel like a bigger fool than she already did at this moment.

HealingGrace: Well, I've fallen in love with a player on the game, and I was just wishing he would come online so we could talk. It is the strangest thing, the attraction and connection between us. Now he is talking of quitting the game, and I can't figure out why.

Karmagirl: Does Theo76 know that you feel this way?

HealingGrace: No, it isn't my game husband I'm talking about.

Karmagirl: Oh, well, I still know how you feel. I've fallen in love with my game husband. I feel like he is with me all the time, and when I'm working I can sometimes feel his touch. It is very distracting.

But you two are connected on a spiritual level. It stems from a past life … and because of this it's a lot harder to dismiss. This is something that needs to be explored and resolved. Enjoy this phase of the "relationship" because what you are experiencing is real.

So may I ask a question? Is the man in question SINGUR…?

Ella felt a chill go up her spine. She had never mentioned SINGUR's name—maybe Karmagirl was the real thing!

HealingGrace: How did you guess that?

Karmagirl: Lol, I said I'm gifted, remember? I know how you feel. I also know that he's telling the truth when tells you he cares for you. His feelings for you run even deeper than he is willing to admit. In fact, he shares more about himself with you than with anyone else.

HealingGrace: Ok

Ella did not want to seem ungrateful for this girl's reading, but so far she hadn't been overly impressed. Or maybe she was just bitter and depressed about what SINGUR had written.

Karmagirl: I feel that between you and SINGUR … something unexpected will happen. Don't assume that this situation has no potential. You two were brought together so that a resolution can occur … just trust the angels … they will give you your answer.

HealingGrace: May I ask you what you do for a living?

Karmagirl: I am a medical student. I live in Portugal. I'm very busy, but I am on this game because I love Mathew. He lives in Croatia. We are planning to meet for real in Italy over my holiday.

HealingGrace: Interesting, I am a physician, too. I hope it works out for the two of you.

Karmagirl: Thank you!

Ella sat back, feeling a little bit better despite her skepticism about Karmagirl's "gift." She was about to sign off when she heard the computer beep again.

Karmagirl: Oh, by the way, as far as this Jasmine is concerned, her affection for SINGUR is more a case of possession than love.

Ella gasped. How could Karmagirl know all of these things? In the end, she thought sadly, it didn't matter. The unavoidable truth was that Jasmine was with SINGUR, and Ella was thousands of miles away with only a vision to keep her company.

*March 24, 2012*

Ella had always been careful to privately message SINGUR, rather than on the public game forum. He was, after all, game married to Jasmine, and gamers often took such relationships seriously. Besides, Ella also believed that Jasmine probably had feelings for him in "real life." This had been confirmed by Karmagirl. Ella often found herself becoming jealous over his notes to Jasmine—they were so romantic and seductive. Then she'd remind herself that she was the one who was married, and not just in a game.

Ella had never had any direct contact with Jasmine; in fact, she didn't even think Jasmine knew she existed. So she was shocked when she received a friend request from her. She didn't want to accept, but did anyway; if she ignored or rejected the request it would look odd. Barely two minutes later, her computer beeped with a private message. Ella's heart skipped; could it be from SINGUR? It wasn't.

Jasmine: What exactly is going on between you and SINGUR?

Just sign off, Ella told herself. You don't owe this woman any explanation, and besides, you don't want to make things difficult for Milan. She maneuvered the cursor over the sign-off button ... then she decided that she was better off answering and being evasive.

HealingGrace: Nothing is "going on." He's just nice to talk to.

Technically, it was the truth, Ella reminded herself.

Jasmine: Did he tell you that he and I are together in real life?

Ella realized that she was shaking her head "no" and placed her shaking hands on the keyboard.

HealingGrace: No

Jasmine: Well, we are. What is it that you are doing here? This isn't a pickup bar or a place to meet singles, you know! This is a game, where people come to relax, have a little fun, and blow off some steam.

HealingGrace: I am not here to pick up anybody. I started playing because my kids play these kinds of games and I wanted to know what they were about.

Jasmine: Well, SINGUR is mine. Remember that.

After that, Ella deleted Jasmine from her friend list. She had enough problems without engaging in a sophomoric pissing contest with a game wife. She knew she shouldn't be so surprised;
Milan *had* told Ella that there was a woman in his life, so why not Jasmine? Karmagirl's last message flitted through Ella's mind: Jasmine did seem to think of him as a possession, and Ella was encroaching on her territory. Meanwhile, she had not heard from him since he had offered to "give her space."
But that didn't matter now. She had to tell him about her exchange with Jasmine.

HealingGrace: Jasmine messaged me. She says she is with you in real life.

Ella pressed send and sat back in the chair, suddenly exhausted. Had she been a fool to believe Milan when he said he loved her? It had felt so real, but maybe it simply exposed all that was missing in her relationship with John, all the affection she had told herself didn't matter because he was such a good, steady man, a reliable partner. Maybe she needed to work on making her real life better, rather than some ethereal tryst with a man thousands of miles away. She signed off the computer and, with a sigh, stood and left the office.

The next day, Ella did not sign onto the computer. Instead, she tried to fill her mind with the day-to-day business of being Manuela Rowan, wife, mother and doctor. She left herself just enough time in the morning to have a shower and a cup of coffee before work. On her way home, she stopped at the market and got all the ingredients for a time-consuming chicken recipe she had always wanted to try but never got around to it. She smiled at the praise from John and the boys when they said it was tasty, then spent the next hour scrubbing the kitchen from top to bottom. She should have been exhausted by the end of the night, but she wasn't.

By 4 a.m., she couldn't stand it anymore. She slid from the bed and went down to the office. She calmly signed on, telling herself she didn't care whether he had replied or not. And when she saw he had, she told herself she didn't care what he said. It doesn't matter, she thought, prolonging the torture and check her emails first. Finally, she clicked on the message.

SINGUR: Whoa, whoa, whoa. It's not like I'm married to her. After Ioana was murdered by that drunk, I was alone for a while. Then I met Jasmine. She is a young but very accomplished and beautiful woman, but like I told you, she isn't in my life every day—YOU are! It is you I am always thinking about. All the time. It is you who I want as my lover, more than anything on this earth.

Ella stared at the screen, knowing that she should just sign off and go back to bed. Her relationship with him, if she could even call it that, defied all logic and common sense, yet it felt more real to her than anything else. Not knowing what to say to him, she forwarded him the messages between herself and Jasmine. He replied with a cryptic, "Okay, thanks."

HealingGrace: I want to tell you about something else that happened—something very strange. This person—she calls herself Karmagirl—wrote me out of the blue, telling me that she has a gift—I guess she is some kind of psychic. Anyway, she told me that I had met someone with whom I have a relationship on a spiritual level. It stems from a past life and that's why it's so hard to dismiss. She said it is something that needs to be explored and resolved. Then she wrote, "Enjoy this phase of the 'relationship', because what you are experiencing is real."

Ella was surprised when a few minutes later she received Milan's response:

SINGUR: Don't tell me this! It scares me.

HealingGrace: Really? I wouldn't have thought you'd feel that way. Aren't you the least bit curious about whether she's right about us?

SINGUR: NO, I AM NOT! And I want nothing to do with Karmagirl.

Ella stared at the screen, more confused than ever.

She had figured Milan would jump at the chance to get answers about what might be happening between them. Besides, he had seemed so open to metaphysical topics. His reaction just didn't make sense. She needed someone to talk to, someone objective, and open-minded. She decided to make an appointment with a psychic. As if on cue, she received a message from Karmagirl. She asked how Ella was doing and even included her personal email in case she needed moral support. When Ella said she was considering a psychic, Karmagirl replied, "Now listen to me, OK? You are to listen to your own instinct when you visit the reader … OK … You doubt yourself because you are seeking answers that you don't need right now. Just flow with it, OK … the answers will come to you … in time … when you are ready to accept them. P.S. Your secret is safe with me."

***

For the next few days, Ella and Milan kept their correspondence light. Given his previous reaction, Ella didn't mention that she'd heard from Karmagirl again. Instead, she asked him when his birthday was (it was May 29), and where he was traveling to next. His travel schedule had always been a safe topic for them, as well as a great way for Ella to learn more about him. He told her he was headed to Brussels, but not for his job. He was going there to apply for funding for an orphanage. The knowledge that he helped these children touched Ella to the core, especially given the fact that she and her sister had been adopted. It lent credence to all she believed to be true about Milan.

March 27, 2012

The following night, Ella awoke from a dream, sweating and agitated. She had been with Milan in a German hotel. They were getting along just fine, each just doing their own thing. Then he had yelled at her, "Get out! GET OUT!" She didn't feel physically threatened, but she was shocked and hurt by the sudden change in him. In all the time they had been communicating he had never even so much as raised his voice; now, he sounded positively enraged.

"Okay," she had muttered tearfully, *"if that's what you want."* As she headed toward the door, it occurred to her that she had no purse, no identification, no money, and no coat. It was brutally cold, and she was clad only in a thin dress. She couldn't speak German, and she didn't know how she would communicate with a taxi driver, or even pay for a plane ride home … and that was when she woke up.

Two days passed without a message from Milan, and the angst and heartache was nearly unbearable, as if someone had stabbed her, then slowly twisted the knife to prolong her suffering. She kept replaying the dream over and over in her mind. It had been so vivid, right down to his slight German accent; Milan's accent always changed, depending on what country he was in. She had always found it to be one of the oddest things about their relationship.

That night, as she climbed into bed, her reply, "Okay, if you want me to get out, then I will…" was on a running loop in her mind. John lay next to her, snoring lightly, and Ella stared at him for a long time, consumed with loneliness. Finally, she fell into a fitful sleep.

This time, the dream began in the house where they had first been together—his house in Romania. She had two suitcases, and she was packing her few pieces of clothing, along with toiletries, makeup and the gifts he had given her. When she was done, she closed up the cases and set them by the front door.

Despondent and standing in the entryway, she saw the front door open. Milan walked in and went directly to her, gently clasping her arms with his hands. No words were said, but he stared deep into her eyes. His were saying, *"Please don't go,"* and *"I love you,"* and *"I'm sorry,"* all at once.

She looked down at her feet, still feeling raw and wounded. She had been grief-stricken all day long. Didn't he know she was in unbearable pain? She would leave if that was what he truly wanted, because she truly loved him.

He lightly cupped her chin and raised her face towards his. Then, staring into her eyes again, he took her hand and led her to the couch in the living room. He moved close to kiss her on the lips, but she turned her head away, thinking, *"Sex doesn't fix everything, you know!"*

He softly touched her leg and told her he loved her, and that he didn't want her to go. He said he was frustrated because he was trying to work, and all he could hear was her voice inside his head. He had just wanted her out of his head, just for a little while, so he could think.

Her eyes met his, and looked searchingly into them.

This seemed to be the truth. He attempted to kiss her again, and this time her lips met his. Slowly but insistently, he eased her back on the couch and began removing her clothing. Ella's resistance melted away as they made love. It felt so good to be in his arms again. She felt pleasure, but more than that, she felt relief.

The next day, Ella needed three cups of coffee to get ready for work, and another two to keep her alert throughout the day. Still, she couldn't resist checking the computer before she turned in for the night.

SINGUR: I felt like you were here ... but I think I came too late to see you online. It's so frustrating when I'm on the move, because I can't talk to you as often as I'd like, but I know it's even worse for you when you're waiting for an answer to a question.

When you feel like I'm mad, angry (btw, I do not anger easily, and even when this happens, it never lasts long) ... or something ... give me two minutes and don't wait for me to talk, 'cause then I just try to find answers ... nothing more. After that, I'm going to give myself to you, and we can talk about anything, good or bad. I'll always tell you what I am thinking and feeling.

Right now I am in Germany, and I'll be here for the next two days or so. Maybe longer, it depends how fast I work. Yes, I've been very busy with work, but I am always here for you.

Ella felt as though a large rock had been removed from her chest, yet she also felt confused. Clearly her dream hadn't completely been off the mark, for he was in Germany. She heard the beep, letting her know that he'd written more.

SINGUR: …and now I must say that I feel like an idiot. I should have been more open to what Karmagirl told you, if only because you were so interested in it. I guess I wanted to figure out how I felt about us before hearing someone else's opinion on it. But you know what? I love you, baby … and even I don't know why. The point is, I've stopped asking myself "why" because I don't care about the answers.

*Yes, you should have been more receptive,* Ella thought, happy yet not willing to completely let it go just yet. She told him about the dream she'd had, when he had ordered her out of the hotel room.

HealingGrace: So, if I understand you correctly, you were thinking GET OUT, as in, GET OUT OF MY HEAD because you wanted to focus on your work, and I somehow got the message to literally get out?
SINGUR: Yes, that is all I meant to say. I love you, Ella, I really do.

Ella sighed. She couldn't remember a time when she had felt more completely and utterly alone. She had no one to talk about Milan to … *except Milan*. She hadn't made the appointment with the psychic yet, and while she told herself it was because she had just been too busy, she knew she was just really afraid they were going to tell her she was nuts, that Milan was just a figment of her imagination—or worse—that he had been lying to her the whole time. Out of desperation, she wrote Karmagirl, who immediately sensed SINGUR'S distrust for her. "He is just afraid of the truth," she told Ella, "because then he may have to change his life for you. Just hang in there—he'll come around."

With all her heart, Ella wanted to believe that Karmagirl was right. But it was becoming harder and harder to face the future. After all, what kind of future could she really have with Milan? She played countless scenarios in her mind, and they all seemed to end with her broken heart. It must have been on his mind too, because they next day she received a message that made her fears all the more real.

SINGUR: We never got to finish discussing Jasmine, and I need you to understand. When you came into my life, Jasmine was already there. I said that I love her, in my way ... and yes, each relationship, each person, is different. Maybe one day I'll make her my wife in "real life," or maybe not. My heart is still in the process of healing after Ioana's loss, and it's still pretty hard for me to even accept Jasmine's love. She waits for months on end, just to receive a little attention from me.

Anyway, I just wanted to be perfectly honest with you. Someday, I will get married in real life ... after all, I have a life. What should I do? It may be Jasmine, it may be some other woman, but there will be a wife one day. Yeah, I am not perfect ... I love two women, in different ways.

As both a scientist and an intuitive, Ella was well aware of the never-ending battle between the human mind and the human heart. However, this battle had never been so clear as in this moment, when she read Milan's words. Rationally, she knew he was just being honest, and that, under the circumstances, she had no right to demand his fidelity. He was young, passionate and virile; of course, he would be with other women, and would most likely get married one day, just as she was married to John. Too bad being rational didn't make it hurt any less.

The computer beeped, and when Ella read his next message, it was as if he had been reading her mind.

SINGUR: Do you think that it is easy for me to "see" and know that you are with your husband?

HealingGrace: I had no idea how you felt about my husband, you haven't said anything other than he seems like a nice guy. He doesn't abuse me. He loves me, like he loves his mother, I guess. If I didn't have kids, I'd have already tried to fly to you in real life. Bad and shameful, I know. Plus you don't have to see me post love letters to him, or him to me, since that just never happens. Even my game husband isn't all that romantic, lol.

She knew she shouldn't remark on Jasmine; sure, Ella didn't like her, but that could very well be simple jealousy.

And perhaps that's why she couldn't resist a small jab.

HealingGrace: Can you feel this, the tears running down my face? The heartbreak of all this does remind me why I chose to marry John. Maybe there isn't passion, there's no soaring bliss, but there aren't any heart-wrenching moments either, no highs or lows. Good night.

*March 31, 2012*

The next morning, Ella could barely open her eyes; not just because she was exhausted, but because they felt as though they were filled with wet sand. She had spent the better part of the night sobbing soundlessly, her chest contracting painfully, so as not to wake John. Still, he had woken at some point and asked her what was wrong. When she replied with a curt "nothing," he didn't press her.

Luckily, Ella had never been one to wallow in her sorrows, and that wasn't going to change now. She allowed herself five more minutes in bed, then she sat up, swung her legs over the side and headed for the bathroom. When she looked in the mirror, she was reminded of all that had changed since meeting Milan. Gone was the cool, collected Dr. Manuela Rowan; she had been replaced by a tear-stained, lovesick mess.

SINGUR: Your note made me very sad, my love, not because of what you are feeling now, but for what you have settled for in your marriage. You deserve better. Anyway, I just wanted to wish you a wonderful day.

Ella felt a rush of anger when she read the note. Who was he to judge how she had lived her life? How she had chosen her husband? At least she had committed to something, and whatever his faults, John was a good man and a good father. Then, realizing that this was more about her internal struggle than any she with Milan, she took a few deep, calming breaths.

HealingGrace: Well, thank you, I wish you a wonderful day, or night, too. How are you doing? I have so much I'd like to talk to you about. Are you in a hotel in Oslo, my love? Is it small, and sparse and cold? It doesn't matter—I'll still wish I were there with you. I'm going crazy trying to understand what is happening here, and I've set up an appointment with a psychic. The soonest she could see me is April 25th.

SINGUR: I hope she has some answers for you—for us.

HealingGrace: I hope so too. I have been thinking a lot about my beliefs, and what I hold dear. When I said the only thing stopping me from getting on a plane to see you was my children, I think that was false. I would never, as a married woman, jump on a plane and meet another man, even if it was someone I loved.

But even as she typed the words, Ella wondered whether

she even believed them. Her relationship with Milan had forced her to reexamine everything she ever believed about life, and herself. She used to believe that if two people were into each other, they didn't notice anyone else; if they did, it was a sure sign that the relationship was over. Now, she had a whole other life separate from the one she shared with John. But did that mean she wanted to end her marriage? She didn't know. The only thing she was sure of these days was that she loved Milan, and would continue to love him, even if he too got married.

HealingGrace: I enjoy this thing we have, whatever it is. It makes me happy. When I am "with" you, I feel complete. I haven't felt that way before. I don't let people know who I am. Yet, somehow, you seem to know. As long as we do not meet in person, I don't feel I'm cheating on my husband. I have a lot more to say, but I have to go to work now … and I really hope I get to see you today or chat with you online. All my love, Ella.

SINGUR: I was working all day, then I went shopping, got a haircut, and now I'm ready to jump into a tuxedo and go to the opera. And through it all, all I can think about is you. I wanted to tell you this, my love, so you are not hurt by what I am about to say. It seems like you think too much about my life, my time, and especially my future. Why? Both of us knew from the beginning that we would never meet in real life, so what is the problem?

HealingGrace: Yeah, I think too much, because you

have turned my life upside down. On the outside it is perfect, but it is missing so much, and all that is missing, I find in you. I wish I were going to the opera with you tonight. You are living the life I want to be living. And since I cannot, I think too much. Have fun tonight, my love. But I can still "come" to your hotel room, can't I? Love and much more, Ella

*April 1, 2012*

HealingGrace: Good morning, Milan. I sensed you last night, between 1:30–3:30 a.m., and these feelings were coming through: possession, love, passion, frustration, and blame. Then I could see you. You were on top of me, making love with me, but when I sensed you blaming me for causing all this frustration, I hit you in the chest with my fists. Then you laughed and agreed not to blame me. How could you blame one magnet for attracting another? All my love, Ella

SINGUR: Yes, my sweet love … it was exactly what I felt. I could not hide my frustration and I could not stop to ask myself, "Why?" I can understand why you need me but I can't understand why I need you. I needed an answer. I felt so strongly the pounding of your fists on my chest … and then … you just brought me back to reality and made me remember why and how I love you. I'm still in Oslo and want to stay until tomorrow. I'll stay these days, because I need to breathe and I want to see other things here. Monday, I have to be in London for one day, and then … I'll see where I'm going. I LOVE YOU, Milan

HealingGrace: Ha, well there is a bit of irony. It is easier for me to understand why you need me. I can warm your icy heart, but when the time comes that you meet a good woman, I can easily disappear. I cannot put any expectations on you. I can only give you my unconditional love.

When we first began to write, I thought it was just a little harmless flirtation, a diversion. Once I discovered that you didn't measure up to my husband, I would appreciate him more, without having actually gone out into the world and "cheated." You, my love, failed your job quite miserably, for you have only shown me what is lacking in John.

The rest is still a mystery to me … the feeling of being hit by lightning when you said your first "hello" … hardly knowing you, yet caring that you stayed in the game, feeling your body actually touch mine, your lips, and then your hands. Now being able to see you, like a spirit and sometimes even a solid form! My head and chest feel a strange rush when your ideas are coming in. I was not looking for this, I know I wasn't, because I didn't even know such things existed, and it only makes me very confused and happy and miserable all at the same time.

I love you, and it would be simpler if I didn't, but I really do. I just remembered the other part of last night. You went straight to it … and I remember saying, "Hey Milan, what happened to our foreplay?" But then you more than made up for it afterwards—after the getting hit in the chest part, that is. Love, M<3

# CHAPTER FIVE

*April 2, 2012*

The following Sunday, Ella awoke slowly, like one does after a long, wonderful sleep. Smiling, she stretched out on the bed, barely noticing that John wasn't there. This was the most rested she had felt in some time. Suddenly, the smile froze on her face and she sat up straight in bed. The reason she had slept so well was that she had not been with Milan.

Forcing down the panic that threatened to rise up in her throat, she got out of bed, slipped into her robe and headed to the computer. John had taken the boys for their tennis lesson, and the house was quiet except for the creaking of the wooden stairs under Ella's feet. *This doesn't mean anything,* she told herself, and *there is no reason to worry.* She continued to tell herself this as she booted up the computer, cursing it for not moving fast enough, and signed onto the game. When she saw Milan had left her a message, the feeling of relief was so overwhelming that it frightened her more than the panic had. Her heart raced even faster when she saw that he was still online.

SINGUR: Hi, baby. I just arrived at the hotel and am a little tired, but I wanted to tell you to have a great day.

Ella typed quickly, worried that he would sign off before they could chat. She hated it when she had to wait for a reply. It was even worse on the weekends, when John and the kids were in and out and she couldn't spend all her free time on the computer.

HealingGrace: I didn't feel you at all last night, where were you? Were you working?

She pressed send, then instantly regretted it, thinking she sounded desperate; or worse, like a nag.

SINGUR: Yes, I was working … for a while. I don't know, baby, everything is new to me/us … I guess I was just feeling some pressure, hearing about how you need me and how you compare me to your husband. But I do miss you and love you. Enjoy your Sunday.

Ella sat back, a bit stung by his words. If anyone were an open book in their "relationship", it was her. Would he disappear every time she opened up to him about her feelings, about her life? She was about to sign off and go make breakfast when she realized he was typing another message.

SINGUR: I don't know why, but I feel compelled to draw you—your face, your body. This is strange and I'm asking myself why, but I get no answer. It doesn't fit with my style, because I only draw in black and white and you are full of color. Hmm … what does this mean? M<3

Ella snorted. Case in point, she thought, for she'd had no idea that he drew at all. And why did he always assume that she had the answers?

HealingGrace: I have no idea, but I have decided to put all my questions about us on hold until I speak to that psychic on the 25th. Do you prefer that I not reveal anything further personal about myself? Because if you do, I can try to be more close-mouthed. It's just that I feel like we are spending so much time together, it seems natural to share things with you. I have no idea what you can "sense" about me, because you've been pretty quiet on that subject—on a lot of subjects. I didn't even know you're an artist. I am happy to hear that you see me in color, though.

SINGUR: LOL, I'm not what you would call an artist, just someone who enjoys sketching every now and again. You can tell me whatever you want, and the rest, I'll try to "see" or "feel" for myself. Now, I'm sorry, but I've got some paperwork to go over before I start my day. Talk soon, my sweet love. Milan.

Ella sighed as she signed off the computer. She knew she should have felt reassured by his message, but she didn't. In fact, she was more confused than ever.

*April 3, 2012*

The next morning, Ella again woke a smile on her face, but for a completely different reason. She had spent the night with Milan, and he had been ever more tender and attentive than usual. When she signed onto the game, however, his message was of a completely different tone. In fact, he had never "sounded" like this in all the time she had known him.

SINGUR: When you have a little time, I would like to know what you think about something. I'm back in London and still trying to figure out where I want to spend my Easter. I'm a little … I don't know … tired of it all, I guess. I began to wonder again, where is my place on this earth? I think I am just a little melancholy right now. But everything went well in Brussels, so that is something. Love, M<3

HealingGrace: London is likely always going to be very difficult for you, making you sad and reminding you of what was lost there. You can't be thinking of staying in London for Easter, can you?

SINGUR: I don't know, Manuela. All I do know is that I lost that woman, and for a new beginning, it takes time, I need time.

Ella paused, wondering what he meant. Did he need time to decide how he really felt about her? A question suddenly popped into her head and she typed it before she could change her mind.

HealingGrace: Do you want children?

SINGUR: Of course I want my own kids, but this thing cannot happen overnight! First, I need a woman to accept me exactly how I am, and I'm thinking that will be very hard for that woman, considering that I'll be gone for work most of the time. My kids will need me all the time and I know for that I need to make some compromises in life, but I don't know if I am ready to do that.

Ella felt a tightening in her chest, the one she always felt when he even hinted that there might be another woman he would settle down with. She knew she had no right to feel this way, but she couldn't help it. She saw that he was still typing.

SINGUR: Of course, I would like it if you could be my children's mother, the woman for whom I'll do anything, but you are already married. I was born ten years too late, and now what do I have? I have all and I have nothing!

Even so, I live in this moment and I enjoy what I have, what WE have. I love you unconditionally and I don't expect anything in return. OK, I don't have my own family and children, but the time isn't lost, not yet.

It was if he was reading her mind. For a moment, she got a flash of how the situation must look through his eyes: an unavailable woman, settled with a family half a world away, claiming to love him. He couldn't afford to risk the rest of his life waiting for her to be free, especially since she had never given him reason to hope for such a thing.

SINGUR: Besides, I have already three children that call me Dad. They are not mine, not biologically. I never officially adopted them either—I couldn't because I was unmarried and considered too young. But I did take them out of an orphanage when they were 15-16 years old. I cared for them full-time for years, and now they are at university, but I'm still the only parent they know. I know it isn't the same thing as having your own, but I try my best.

As she read the message, Ella wanted to scream. How could he not have told her such an important thing about himself? Especially after he had found out she was adopted!

SINGUR: I don't want to think about these things right now. All I want to do is kiss your neck. Vampires are originally from Romania, you know. LOL.

For the first time, Ella was glad they communicated through a computer; it made it easier to conceal her frustration at how secretive he was, and how he had gone on to make a joke out of it. Well, two could play at this game.

HealingGrace: Yes, I did know that the legend of vampires originated in Romania. They taught me a reasonable explanation for vampires in medical school. They said that they were people with a metabolic disorder called porphyria, so they craved red meat and couldn't tolerate the sun or their skin would blister. Have a great day, Milan, and I hope you feel better soon. All my love, M<3

*April 4, 2012*

SINGUR: I'm ready now to leave the game, for real this time. We could set up email accounts and use instant messenger to "talk" in real time. I think it is for the best.

Ella's heart skipped a beat as she read the words. Why did he want to leave the game? Did it mean he was leaving Jasmine as well? Why else would he do it? She was afraid to ask.

HealingGrace: Okay, then that's what we will do. I just want you to know that I am grateful to know you, even like this, even though it's far from ideal. My life is still better than it was before "meeting" you, even with all the bizarre questions our relationship raises. I love you, and I would never want you to change who you are. BUT, if I was married to you, and trying to be a doctor and raise kids, I'm sure I would want you home more. Sometimes, I'd even want to travel with you ... unless of course we had small children at home.

Even if you had been born ten years earlier, we would never have met; we only did because of the Internet game.

I know you are busy, and have work to do. When you have time, I want to hear a little about your family. I love you, M<3

SINGUR: I have a nephew, named after me, little Milan. I think maybe I should go home to Romania for Easter. I should do it for him.

If I'm going to talk about my nephew, I have to talk a little bit about my younger sister first. She is ten years younger than me—a very beautiful girl. When she was sixteen, she fell in love with a guy—a bad one—who hung out with a bad group. I didn't know about it. So, one day she runs away with that guy because she knew that nobody would agree with her choice. A whole week, nobody knew anything about her/him, etc. After a week, she called me and told me that she was OK. We spoke a lot, and I met her several times and didn't tell anyone else about it.

I offered my support, as I always did, and finally I asked her if she really wanted that man to be the father of her children. She thought about it a little bit and said, "No, I don't want that." I was going to Italy the next day, and asked her to come with me, take some time to think about what she was doing with her life. She agreed, and that was it.

She lived there for a while with our other sister, and then she met her husband. They got married soon after, and I guess my nephew was a kind of present for me … 'cause I "saved her life." They always said—and I don't know why—that they would want their children to be like me. What can I say? He is a smart kid for his age, a lovely boy and already he has an eye for the girls. I am crazy for him!

HealingGrace: Milan, that is a beautiful story, and you are a man with a very beautiful heart and soul. So, one younger sister lives in Romania, with your nephew and namesake. And you have another sister who lives in Italy?

SINGUR: Yes, we're spread out all over the place, and isn't easy, but we all love each so we make it work.

HealingGrace: I hope you decide to go home to Romania for Easter, see your parents and your sister and her family.

SINGUR: Yeah, I think I will go home for Easter, especially because … well, I believe someone needs me there. I think I will take my car. Two days driving, enough time to think and forget the rest of the world. Speaking of which, I really have to go; I have some things to take care of.

Ella could tell by the abruptness of his message that she had hit a sore spot. His family. The question was, why?

HealingGrace: If I've upset you, I'm sorry. You know my intention isn't to hurt—I'm trying to be helpful.

SINGUR: It's not you, baby, I am not feeling very well tonight ... I don't know what is going on with me. But thank you for trying to help. I love you for it. M<3

As she read the message, Ella felt a sudden tightness in her belly and an ache at her temple.

HealingGrace: Milan, is your stomach hurting? Head aching? I can feel it. Would it be OK if I just lay next to you while you watch your movie, maybe kiss your fingers now and then? In the meantime, maybe this will cheer you up:

Song: "Amazed" by Lonestar.

A few minutes passed, presumably while he listened to song, then she saw that he was typing.

SINGUR: You, baby, YOU are amazing! Hmm ... there are so many things that I want to do right now ... bad things, baby. I love you so much ... but you know that already ... at least I hope you do. That's why I try to tell and show you my feelings every single day. Good night, my love.

HealingGrace: LOL. You say you are going to do bad things, but as far as I'm concerned they have been really, really GOOD. Call them whatever you like, just so long as you keep doing them! Good night.

Ella went to bed early that night, even though she wasn't a bit tired. She slowed as she approached John's study, which was on her way to the staircase. The door was partly ajar, and the room was dark, but for the glow of the television. The volume was turned down low, and was punctuated every few moments by John's brief, nearly humorless chuckle. She stood outside the door, about to go in and at least kiss her husband goodnight. Then the moment was gone and she continued toward the stairs. Milan was waiting.

*April 5, 2012*

The morning had become Ella's favorite part of the day, a time to reminisce about her adventures with Milan, and even pretend she had another life, with him, in that apartment in London. The night before had been incredible, once she had calmed her mind and drifted to the verge of sleep.

She was in the apartment. Usually when Milan had a lot of work to do, she left him alone and did her own thing … reading or exercising. On this night, she had just finished her shower and emerged from the bathroom clad in a new pink lace bra, matching panties, and a white fluffy robe that reminded her of the Easter bunny. Her makeup and hair were done, and she already had her pearl earrings on ... and Playboy bunny ears!

Milan was supposed to be working, but when Ella stepped into the hall, there he was, waiting for her. "I want to sketch you," he said, "maybe paint you too." Thinking he was joking, Ella laughed and shook her head; but then he grabbed her hand and led her to another room. It was filled with art supplies—paints, and pencils and sketchbooks and a palette. Instrumental music played softly in the background and the soft glow of candles illuminated the room.

"Okay, Milan, how would you like me?"

He had cleared the middle of the room, but for an area rug and a big chair. "Over here...," he said, walking over to the spot on the rug. Ella followed, and he gently took the robe off her. He spent a moment, looking her over, then positioned her arms this way and that.

Finally he instructed her to take off the new pink lingerie. Blushing furiously, Ella slowly obliged. When she was completely nude, he had her try a number of different poses ... standing, sitting, on all fours, frontward, and looking over her shoulder with her back to him. He didn't use words so much, but simply touched her; then he would stand back, observe her again as if checking to see if the lighting was right.

Then he began teasing her with the paintbrushes, lightly running the soft bristles over her breasts and nipples—

tickling every part of her.

After a few moments, he positioned her so she was standing on one leg, the other leg bent at the knee with the foot resting up on the chair. Ella covered her breasts with her hands, then looked back over her shoulder at him. "Oh, I like that," Milan purred, "can you hold it for fifteen minutes?"

"Sure, no problem."

"I bet you can't…," he said with a sexy smile.

"Oh really? What would you like to bet? How about a thirty-minute massage? If I can stay like this for fifteen minutes, you will give me a thirty-minute massage, and if I can't then I will give YOU a thirty-minute massage. Do we have a deal?"

He laughed playfully. "Yes, we do."

He ran to the kitchen to grab a timer, setting it for a quarter of an hour. When he came back to the room, he pulled his shirt up over his head and flung it to the corner of the room. "Okay, you can't move," he said, kissing her legs, "unless it is to touch your nipples."

Ella did so, and he got down to the floor, kissing her ankles, and legs, and up, up until he was underneath her … and well surely no one could hold still for fifteen minutes under those circumstances.

The he took off his pants, and they were both nude and sinking to the floor. He was sitting up, and had Ella face him, sitting her down onto his hard cock. Her legs wrapped around him so that their bodies were together. They were kissing and barely moving, yet it was so incredibly intense it took her breath away.

Ella relived the moment while lying in her bed, then again as she typed the words to Milan.

SINGUR: I didn't know why I felt "the need" to paint you today! I thought it might have been on my mind because I had told you about it ... and I do have an easel, brushes and stuff like that here in London. But every time I picked up a brush, I could not. Every time I think of you ... I want to touch you, kiss you and make love to you ... so I forgot about drawing/painting, LOL.

HealingGrace: So I made all the rest up myself? You didn't "feel" or send any of it? Hmmm. That is a more rational explanation than our other experiences. We had talked about it, after all ... did you think of something else and I just didn't "get it"?

SINGUR: Baby, I definitely felt you, and I sent my thoughts also. But I am a little bit confused because it was overlapped with my desire to draw/paint you in the past days, and I thought it was just my own desire, not something you sent me.

HealingGrace: Oh good, because one of the big "wows" for me regarding us is that I really feel it and experience it just like it is real life. From the first time we "connected" ... I remember being so bowled over by how real the dream seemed to be.
The other big "wow" is that I don't feel lonely when we are together. I feel happy and complete and whole—

different from how I normally feel. I'm not saying I walk around depressed all the time, because I certainly don't. I've just always felt like a bit of an outsider, not "like" other people ... until you came along. I don't know why, but even though we're clearly quite different, I also feel like we are somehow very similar. Whatever the case, I love you.

SINGUR: Yes, my love ... that would be how it would be in real life if we were together ... that's why I get so angry sometimes that we cannot be together. But somehow, we are ... I feel like I am yours and you are mine ... it is weird, wonderful and painful at the same time.

And, yes, we are very similar and very different as well. You feel alone or lonely ... I am alone but I never feel lonely. I am like a magnet and sometimes I feel like I am drained of energy, always trying to transform a tear into a smile, tears, pain and suffering that no one can see but me. I always want to see everyone happy. I am always smiling and people have told me that I infected them with my optimism and "good mood." Sometimes I just crave the solitude.

HealingGrace: I am going to enjoy being with you in any way I can, for as long as it may last.

Milan: Then I will do the same. Now, I will be away from computers for a while ... please, my darling, don't think I disappeared on you. You are never far from my thoughts. I love you.   Milan

April 6, 2012

Ella signed onto the game, only to find that Milan had indeed closed out his account. She smiled as she saw that he had also emailed her from a new account created just for that purpose. It was nice to see his real name, staring back at her. The subject line was "test email," and the message was that he was thinking of her skin. He wasn't online, so she wrote him a quick note, asking how he was feeling. She had awoken around midnight with a stomachache. She had a cast iron stomach and felt fine otherwise; she knew immediately that she was picking up on how Milan was feeling. Was he sick? Stressed?

She sent the email and was about to get ready for work when her eye landed on her cell phone, which was on the other side of desk. This is probably a mistake, she thought, as she added the new Gmail account. At least she would know when Milan wrote her, even if she couldn't always answer.

A few hours later, Ella had just finished with a patient when her phone buzzed in the pocket of her white lab coat. She quickly reached for it, her heart leaping in her chest as she saw that he had responded.

Milan: I do NOT want to send you my PAIN … this is the worst part! Sorry, baby. I'll try to stay away from you. I feel fine now, and I am going out for dinner. I will see you later, my love.

"Dr. Rowen, your next patient is waiting in Exam Room 4. Dr. Rowen?"

Ella glanced up from her phone, trying to hide the flash of panic that went through her when she read the words, "stay away from you." The receptionist was looking at her quizzically.

"Yes, thank you, Jane. I'll be there in a moment." Ella called the last words over her shoulder as she headed to the ladies room.

Ella: I don't want you to stay away from me. Please don't even say that. Besides, who's to say I still wouldn't feel your pain anyway? That is what people in love do—they share the pain, as well as the pleasure. I hope you don't mean it. Love, M<3

She paused a moment, then began a new message and wrote in the subject line: Do you feel my pain too?

She slipped her phone back in her pocket and left the bathroom, but he stayed on her mind the rest of the day. The heavy traffic on the way home was actually a relief, for it took her mind from him.

Milan: Yes, I can feel your pain, and I do not wish to add more pain to your life. I won't leave, though, not unless you ask me to. By the way, I have decided to go home for Easter. My mom has been sick, and I hope to make her feel better. I always make her laugh, and then the next second

I'm very serious and I ask her why she is laughing. This is me—funny and serious at the same time. Tomorrow, I'll be ready to go home to Romania ... to my children, family and friends. What are your plans, my love? Love you with all my heart, Milan

Ella: I'm am so glad to hear that you'll be with your family, and I have no doubt that you will bring them joy, as you do me. I saw your serious side from the beginning, but it is really nice to see your fun, playful side, too.

I'm going to relax, and spend time with family. There will be grandparents, cousins, that kind of thing.

But then of course I will "be" with you too. I'm so looking forward to driving across Europe with you. Will you have any kind of Internet connection, though? Oh well, I hope to catch up with you in a little while. Love, Ella

Milan: Oh, my love, I just need to sleep for thirty minutes, then we can go home. I'm really tired, and it was a crazy day. I will be there with you when you need me, and I hope to see/feel you beside me when you are not very busy.

Yeah, it is a long road but I need time to empty my soul and my mind because I'll need of a lot of energy when I am home. I host the holidays, and my home is open to anyone who wants to come. We sing and play a bunch of different games, and there is a lot of noise and chaos. The only time

I have any peace is after everyone else has gone to bed.

But until then ... it is a long road ... I'll write here from my car or wherever. Good night my love ... and see you soon. All my love, M<3

Ella: I'm so glad to hear you'll be in touch from the road. Do you take many photos during your trips? You must see so many wonderful things. For me, it's good night now, and I hope to see you in my dreams. Good night my love, M<3

*April 7, 2012*

The next morning was rather gloomy, matching Ella's mood. She usually looked forward to the holidays—the food, spending time with family—but now all she could think about was Milan, traveling to Romania. She would miss him terribly if he didn't keep in touch while he was away, but she knew she had no right to make any demands on him.

Milan: Hi, my love. Yeah, I guess I can say that I am at home ... or I don't know, it is a strange feeling. Everything seems perfect; the house is decorated, illuminated, warm inside and a lot of surprises from my friends. Yet, here I am, missing you so badly and wanting you to be here. The only woman I want is not with me. The way I am feeling ...

how do you say this in America: fuck me!

When she read the last line Ella laughed out loud. Suddenly, a vision of a quaint neighborhood appeared before her. She watched as Milan got out of his car and walked up to a cozy house. He stepped through the front door, and she saw what he was seeing: a fireplace, made of floor-to-ceiling grayish stones; a bright kitchen, very modern, with a huge, steel refrigerator and windows looking out onto the driveway.

Ella blinked and was back in her room, at her desk, staring at the computer screen. She typed out a reply to Milan, recounting her "vision" of his house in Romania. Then she asked, "Do you believe in past lives?"

Milan: I don't think I have had many lives, just this one. And in this life, I always believed that we are the result of our own choices. But at the same time, life is a mystery and something beyond our knowledge and the power of understanding.

Yes, my fireplace is made of stones, like the pillars of the house and other parts of the outside. My kitchen is bright white ... and I am looking around like a fool right now, seeing my home through your eyes.

Ella: I am a little inclined to believe in past lives. I'm not sure about them, but I wouldn't deny them either. My family is Catholic, and I know reincarnation isn't a part of their belief system (at least, not now—before Constantine it was) but I don't really care, LOL.

I felt like I experienced another time together with you … but I want you to tell me this time what you felt.

Milan: I … we got home. We spent some time on the snow. We made love … outside and inside of the house. After that, I went to store to buy coffee and other stuff, and then we were back in front of the fireplace. I was happy and sad at the same time. We made love on the carpet in front of the fireplace.

Then he begged off, saying he had to tend to his guests. Ella looked at the email, torn between great relief and great anxiety. Milan had validated her vision, yet this only made her sadder. Most women would be thrilled to take a lover, to juggle to separate lives. For her, it was like a looking through a plate-glass window at her destiny, and no matter how she tried, she just couldn't get inside.

# CHAPTER SIX

*April 8, 2012 – Easter Sunday*

Ella leaned the broom against the kitchen counter and ran the back of her hand over her damp brow. In a couple of hours, seventeen guests, mostly John's family, would fill her house for Easter dinner. It was the largest gathering she had hosted in some time, and she would have much preferred to curl up on the couch with a good book. Of course, part of her fatigue had to do with her active "dream life." She could barely suppress her smile at the thought; it would have to get her through the day. It wasn't that she didn't enjoy being around the Rowens—they were a kind, close-knit group. But she couldn't deny that it made her feel guilty, entertaining John's family while she was in love with another man. She heard the boys moving around upstairs, carrying out her orders to clean their rooms. Ella took one last look around the kitchen, then ran up to take a shower.

People started arriving in the early afternoon: John's parents, followed by his two sisters, their husbands and their gaggle of kids. As usual, Ella's mother-in-law made a beeline for the kitchen; it would be her domain for the next several hours. It was annoying sometimes, the way she treated Ella as if she were still a young wife, playing house, but in truth, Ella was grateful that she didn't have to cook. Instead, she was free to make the rounds among her guests. She went going through the motions of a holiday celebration, hugging and kissing and smiling until her face felt tight, but the greater part of her was somewhere else.

After they had stuffed themselves on her mother-in-law's ham and mashed potatoes, the men headed to the den to watch something sports-related on T.V. John's nieces and nephews went upstairs to play, giving the adults a much-needed break. The women remained around the table, catching up on their lives. Ella made idle chitchat, fully aware that she was putting on a show. After all, it wasn't like she could share what had really been going on. Over the years she'd often watched her sisters-in-law and their husbands, holding hands, giving each other affectionate glances, and wondered what they thought of her marriage. Did they notice that she and John barely looked at each other? Did they think it was her fault?

Ella checked on the guys to see if they needed anything, then returned to the table and poured herself a glass of red wine. All in all, the day had gone well, everyone seemed to be having a good time. She took another sip of her wine and felt herself, finally, starting to relax.

She listened to the conversation around her, idly scanning the scene. Suddenly she felt her body stiffen. From her seat she could see into the kitchen, and she saw the transparent image of a man standing in the corner near the pantry. Milan! His form grew clearer, as if the molecules of his body were solidifying right before her eyes. Although he was still transparent, like a phantom or apparition, she could see his face, his black turtleneck, costly black leather jacket and blue jeans. He was leaning back against the wall, with one leg crossed in front of the other. He just seemed to be taking in the whole scene. There was a pleasant smile on his face. His hands were in his jacket pockets.

Then, as if he felt her stare, he turned to look at her. "Hello, my sweet love," he said quietly, his eyes locked onto hers. Ella nearly dropped her wine glass. She looked around to see if anyone else saw him, or her reaction to him, but no one seemed to have noticed. She wanted to go to him but felt cemented to her chair. It wasn't like she could run over to the pantry and say, "What are you doing here?" She glanced around the room and when her gaze returned to him, Milan was gone. Rattled to the core, she suddenly couldn't wait for everyone to leave.

"Ella?"

With a start, she realized her sister-in-law was speaking to her; she had a strange, almost worried, look on her face.

"Sorry." Ella shrugged and held up the near-empty wine glass. "Can't handle the booze anymore."

The women burst into laughter, and Ella sighed inwardly with relief.

*April 9, 2012*

Ella didn't sleep a wink all night; even the red wine didn't have its usual sedative effect. She closed her eyes and took deep, slow breaths, anything to relax her body so she wouldn't disturb John. She glanced at the clock—3 a.m.—soon it would be time to get up for work. She turned on her side to look at her husband. His profile, still proud and handsome, was outlined in the beam of moonlight streaming in through the window. She realized it was the most attention she had paid to him in months. Seeing his family today had reminded her of how estranged they had become. She didn't know what had happened between them; all she knew was that it happened long before she met Milan.

She was just starting to doze off when she felt John slip from the bed. As soon as he left for his run, she headed for the computer. Her hands nearly shaking with anticipation, she logged into the computer, thrilled to see that he was online. She didn't even bother to email him, and went directly to the instant messenger:

Ella: Were you at my house yesterday?

A second later, she heard the telltale ding.

Milan: Yes, I was at the dinner party. It was so strange, I wanted to see what the deal was with your husband, and suddenly there I was, in your kitchen. I saw your home, and all your guests. I can tell he loves you. He is too American for me, though. I wanted to see your children too. It was all very nice.

Despite her continued confusion, Ella smiled.

Ella: Yes, he is very American. I was worried when we first met that I was too American for you.

Ella thought about how he looked standing in her kitchen, in his European, clearly very expensive designer clothes. It must have seemed so "quaint" to him, so provincial.

Milan: You are perfect, my love. I love everything about you. You are not too American for me. And I am glad John has been there to take care of you. All my love, Milan.

After adding that he some business to attend to, he signed off, leaving Ella inexplicably sad. She knew she should be touched by his words about John, but they only seemed to emphasize that they would never be together in real life. She just wished she could talk to someone, anyone, who could help. Unfortunately, everyone she knew would have her locked up if they heard her story. She paused for a moment; actually, there was one person.

For the first time in a long time, she signed onto the game and wrote to Karmagirl:

HealingGrace: Please help me, I'm so confused. I'm

married in real life, and I have children, and somehow I've completely fallen in love with SINGUR. I've never asked him for a photo, partly because I see him so clearly in my head, but mostly because it seemed like it is one step closer to cheating on my husband. I don't want to be a cheater, ever! SINGUR and I are not talking as much now because he's busy traveling, but I still feel so out of control, maybe ever more so.

Ella finished the note and clicked send right away so she couldn't change her mind. Then with a sigh, she got up and went about her day. That was on a Monday, and Karmagirl didn't reply for two whole days.

Karmagirl: Hi there … oh please forgive me for not replying to your note sooner. It's just that I am in the middle of my exams and doing a rotation at a local hospital as well. I'm exhausted.

HealingGrace: That's okay, if anyone can understand what that's like, it's me. I just wanted someone to vent to. And tell you that I've made an appointment with a psychic on April 25th. Maybe she can give me some answers.

Karmagirl: That's great about the appointment, but remember what I said. You must listen to your own instinct. We all want instant gratification, but it is often best to just go with the flow. The answers will come to you only when you are ready to accept them.

PS: Thank you for coming into my life, HealingGrace, you have made me feel "normal." I know what you are going through, because I am living it as well. Don't give up on your dream ... leave SINGUR to his own torment. He misses your companionship ... and still feels you around him.

Ella thanked her and wished her good luck at school, then signed off, grateful for even this small measure of comfort.

*April 10, 2012*

She felt even better when later that day she received a note from Milan. It was just a hello, but it did much to ease the nerves in her stomach, and the empty ache she always felt when he was away too long.

Ella: The car we drove from London to Romania ... was it a black Porsche? I earn a good living, but nothing like you, it seems. Now I see why you can be aloof; you are hunted by gold-digging females, lol. How is your day going?

Milan: Hi, my love. My day has been wonderful. This morning I picked up my nephew at his mother's house and we had a great time together. I am going to take him home now.

Yeah, my Porsche is black ... but as for the women, who knows for sure what they want with me? It does not matter, because I am immune to their charms. I love only you, with all my heart. Besides, if anyone would be the hunter, it would be me, LOL.

As she read the last line, Ella felt a tightening in her gut. What did he mean, he would be the hunter? Was this all some sort of game to him? She took a few deep breaths, debating how she should respond, then decided on the easy route.

Ella: Well, I'm happy you had the chance to spend the time with your nephew. I know how important your family is to you.
Something new happened when I was with you this morning. It was early, just after 4am, when I smelled fresh coffee—two different times! I've never smelled anything associated with you.
It wasn't all about the coffee, though, lol. All I have to say is, if I turn up pregnant in the next month or so, I KNOW THE BABY IS YOURS, LOL. That would definitely be more bizarre than what has happened so far! All my love, Ella

*That's great, Ella,* she chided herself as she pressed send. *Mention a baby to man you've never met, and he may "hunt" women while he's jet-setting around the world.*

Milan: Oh, my love ... everything about this is so bizarre, I don't believe anything could surprise me now. I know you were joking about being pregnant—and perhaps letting me know you are not intimate with your husband...? I know I have no right to hope that this is the case, but I do anyway. And I cannot allow myself to think about a baby, because you know how much I want this thing to be true. I try to enjoy every moment because we don't know what will be tomorrow.

Ella sat back in her chair, not knowing what to think. She knew he loved her—or at least he believed he did. But have a family with her? Did he dream about that, as she did? Did he even know what that meant? It was one thing to spend glorious nights together in some kind of dream state; it was entirely another to live the day-to-day. Besides, what did it matter, anyway? It wasn't like she was free. Without replying to his message, she logged off the computer and put her head in her hands.

"Ella, are you okay?"

Ella jerked up her head to see John, standing in the doorway of her office, wearing a tracksuit and a concerned expression. She felt the blood rushing to her face, as though he had caught her kissing another man. Or maybe it was just because she couldn't remember the last time she'd felt like John was really seeing her.

"Um ... yes, yes," she said quickly, "of course I'm okay."

She laughed awkwardly to cover up the brusqueness of her tone. It didn't work. She saw John's mouth tighten; it was almost imperceptible, but she saw it.

"Oh, well, I'm sorry to bother you."

"You didn't bother me, John. What's up?"

John looked like he was about to say something, then changed his mind. The concern was gone, replaced by a mask of indifference. "Nothing. It was nothing."

With that, he turned and left. Ella sighed. Now she had two unreadable men to deal with. She grabbed the book off her desk and opened it, hoping it could give her the answers she so desperately needed. When she was done, she felt ready to answer Milan.

Ella: Remember that book on spirituality I was reading? Well, I finally finished it. It says the pain of this weird relationship we're in and the roller-coaster ride of intense emotions we're experiencing … it is because you can feel my emotions and I yours, and so everything is magnified, making us feel crazy.

Anyway, it says that when two souls are connected but cannot physically be together, Reiki might be able to help. I don't know much about Reiki, but I'd be willing to look into it. I love you, but this pain … sometimes it's so bad I feel it physically, in my heart; in my stomach … Do you know anything about chakras? I didn't, but the book talked a lot about that too. Is this all too hokey for you? If so, I'm sorry.

Milan: No, *I* am sorry, baby, but I do think it's, how you

say, hokey. Maybe it's because I don't care what any book says about how I feel. It's useless. I love you.

Ella: I understand what you're saying, and I love you, too. But the Reiki ... the book says if we decide to not communicate anymore, it can help heal our souls of the pain of separation. It's not an option I want to dwell on, but it is an option.

Milan: I love you for telling me this, trying to save me pain, but I do not wish to hear about this option. How can I think about separating from you? I have to go to a party tonight and I have a headache already, just wishing you could be here with me. I know I should be grateful that I know you at all, but right now all I can think is, this is not fair! Now, I must go, my love, but I will write more tomorrow.

As she signed off the computer that night, Ella could not deny her relief. Maybe Reiki was a cure, but if it meant losing Milan, it would be worse than the disease. She slipped into bed next to John and closed her eyes, but it took forever to fall asleep. Suddenly, she was drifting over a crowd of people. They were expensively dressed in gowns and tuxes, and the room was richly decorated in dark wood and tapestries. The place had a distinctly European feel to it, but it was the Europe of another time. She knew Milan was there somewhere, she could feel him, but no matter how hard she searched, he was nowhere to be found.

*April 11, 2012*

Ella: What kind of party did you attend last night? It felt very stuffy, somewhere that I would be out of place.

Milan: The party was very stuffy. It was to celebrate a new building that has been opened in town—actually, a wing at the hospital for a new therapy. I am always bored at those things, but last night was worse because I wanted you there. You could never be out of place. Anywhere I go, you are welcome. Think of me as your passport, LOL.

That night, Ella was so exhausted she fell asleep as soon as her head hit the pillow. She knew from the moment the dream began that it was a real dream, not a visitation with Milan, and that knowledge was the only thing that saved her, for she was watching him and another woman.
 First they were arm in arm, dressed in fine clothes and walking down a cobblestone street; then they were in a hotel room and he was slowly undressing her. With every bit of her strength, Ella pulled herself out of her sleep. Her face was wet with tears. When she went to the computer the next morning, there was an email from him, marked urgent.

*April 12, 2012*

Milan: Hi, baby. I'm home. I have a strange feeling and I don't know what exactly it is. Is something wrong? Did something happen to you?

Ella: No, nothing happened. I just had a terrible dream last night. You were with Jasmine … still. And you were … well, like I said, it was a terrible dream. I crave you like I crave a drug, and in the dream, Jasmine was getting my "fix." But I will try to stay happy and not worry about things I cannot control. Love, Ella

PS: Are you still in Romania? For some reason, I've been thinking about Geneva. It is weird, but I feel like I have an apartment there.

Milan: I felt that, your jealousy. I cannot be happy when you are hurt, my love. But I also thought all day of Geneva … and now that you say it, I feel that you have an apartment there. How bizarre is that? I FEEL THE SAME THING!

Ella: I guess there is no lying to you, lol, not that I would ever want to. This last week, more than ever before, I could only find fault with my husband. Little things that he has said or done for years, but that I now blow out of proportion. I have no loving words for him, and we never, ever touch. It's been like that for a long time, and I always blamed him, but now I see it is my fault too. I'm in love with you, and you get it all, I guess.

Do you have anyone you can talk to … about us? I have a friend, Shelby. She doesn't know about you yet, but I think she would understand how we feel. Once we were talking about relationships and she compared them to a pair of gloves. "Once you've worn a pair that fit you so perfectly, no other gloves feel right. They just annoy you." Now I think I finally understand what she was talking about. It's why some women choose to stay single after their great love dies. I never got that before, but I think I do now.

Milan: I think your friend Shelby is very wise. :)

Ella: What I really want to say, what I have been dying to ask you is, if I weren't married, would we really have a chance together? Or would all the other stuff still get in the way? The book said that when people are in our situation, one of them is usually in a safe, secure but unfulfilling marriage, and that would be me. It also said that one of the partners is often a runner, unable to cope with the intensity of the feelings. I guess that would be you, so I'll just keep hanging out by your side, phantom-like, as long as you'll have me there. Many kisses, Ella

Milan: Why do you think I try to keep my mind so busy, because if I stop and think about my life I will be incredibly pissed off. With one hand, it gives me everything and with the other hand, it takes it away. When my fiancée died, I worked very hard to accept my fate and go on, like everyone told me. Now, when I found the woman I'm looking for in life ... This must be a really bad joke.

Yes, Ella, if you weren't married you would be the woman of my life and my wife. I am sorry if I can't always be here when you need me, but that does not mean I am not always thinking of you and wishing you were here. Never forget this. I love you so much, Milan.

Ella: I guess I'm not even asking if you would make me your wife, because it seems so extreme for two people who have never really met and who have known each other such a short time (but I love that you said it anyway). I hadn't planned on having such a serious conversation today, but you can see how well that turned out.

But if I am going to pine away for you all the time, I had to know if you saw some possibility of our being together. If I wasn't married, bearing in mind that I have 15-year-old twin sons, and it is quite doubtful given my advanced years, LOL, that I could safely give you children. And I KNOW you want children....

These are things I think about, my love. The work part, I've already figured out. I think I could get a medical license in Switzerland and work there part time, something like that. But then I think about my age, and how important having your own flesh and blood children are to you—that's what worries me. Love, Ella

Milan: Don't ever worry that you can't give me what I want. YOU are what I want. In my mind, the only problem is that you are married.

Ella was about to sign off when she saw that she had a message from Karmagirl. She clicked it open, her mouth curving into a smile as she read it.

Karmagirl: Just a little something that I find helpful when I've lost my bloody mind! You see, I completely understand what you are going through.

*Mantra*
*Bring me Love and Passion. Excite the heart of my soul mate and draw him swiftly to my side. My magnetic love pull will make others slaves to my passionate desires within. Bring me a willing lover to satisfy the needs of my body. I command the invisible forces around me to go now, and shape the future such that my lover turns to me in fervor and in love.*

I thank the Universe for sending you to me. Now I don't feel so crazy, LOL. Talk soon, stay focused and clear-headed. Trust your intuition … OK? Lida

Ella typed off a quick thank you, moved by Karmagirl's kindness while at the same time recognizing its futility. She had love and passion, and the heart of her soul mate was quite excited already. But she couldn't, for the life of her, begin to imagine that he would ever be at her side.

*April 13, 2012*

Milan: I woke up very hungry this morning … must be from the "workout" we had last night. How are you, my love?

As if on cue, Ella's stomach rumbled. Was she feeling his hunger, she wondered, or her own? It seemed another line between them had blurred, another line between dreaming and waking. They had shared an amazing time the night before, maybe the best ever. She ran her fingers along her lips; they actually felt raw and slightly swollen.

Ella: I am as good as I can be. You, sir, are an amazing kisser, and just thinking about it makes my entire body shiver. But, before this relationship goes any further, I have something very important to tell you.…

She clicked send and sat back, awaiting his rely.

Milan: WHAT IS IT?

Ella smiled. He always seemed so self-assured, so sure of her. Had she made him nervous?

Ella: Well … I can't cook. I never learned how.

Milan: That is it? LOL!! :) I thought you were going to tell me something really serious, although I cannot imagine that you could tell me anything that would scare me away. I can't cook either, but it is no problem. That's why God created restaurants, yes?

Ella: Yes, that's how I've always looked at it, too, LOL. I just know that a lot of men fantasize about the woman who looks good in lingerie and "sizzles" in the kitchen. I may be doing okay with the first part, but definitely not the second. Just thought you should know.

Milan: You are much more than OK, my love. You are the most beautiful woman I have ever seen. So never worry about disappointing me. This is not possible. You are always on my mind, when I am on a plane or meeting with my partners. Especially when I am speaking to a woman, because I am as you say, hunted, sometimes. All I can think about is how she is not you.

People come, people go, people talk, people laugh ... I'm looking through them. I can't hear and I can't understand what they say because my thoughts are full of you....

Ella didn't know whether to laugh or cry. It had been his greatest declaration yet, the greatest glimpse into his real life. But how long before he did fall for one of those young, undoubtedly beautiful women? She almost wrote something to that effect, but stopped herself. What would it accomplish? He would just deny it and she would look like a jealous hausfrau.

Ella: Ahh ... that sounds like me at one of my parties. Easter with John's family ... well, it was hard. But you didn't answer my question. Do you have anyone to confide in?

Milan: No, no one.

Ella: Not even your sister? I thought maybe when you saw your family for the holidays...? But I guess you wouldn't tell. I mean, it's not like they would understand, unless they happen to know what a "soul pull" feels like. Besides, when we first met on the game you told me that you are alone, but not lonely.

That day had been less than a year ago, but it felt like a lifetime. Ella summoned a mental picture of herself back then: a successful, attractive, seemingly-happily-married woman. An empty shell.

Milan: That was true, until I met you ... I am lonely for you.
But as I said, I don't talk to anyone about myself or my issues, because nobody can tell me what is the best for me. They can give advice, but in the end, the decision is mine. Do you understand? I love you so much, M<3

Ella: Yes, I do understand. It's just so hard to know what is real and what isn't in this relationship of ours, and sometimes I crave reassurance. But I do know that it's easier for me to picture a life with you than it is to picture a life without you. All my love, Ella

Ella was about to log off the computer when she remembered Karmagirl's mantra. She printed it out, then laid it slowly on the desk and focused her mind.

*"Bring me Love and Passion. Excite the heart of my soul mate and draw him swiftly to my side. My magnetic love pull will make others slaves to my passionate desires within. Bring me a willing lover to satisfy the needs of my body. I command the invisible forces around me to go now, and shape the future such that my lover turns to me in fervor and in love."*

Her heart pounded stronger and faster, louder and stronger; then in her mind's eye, she began to visualize. Now she could see him in the living room of his large house ... he is wearing jeans, and a tee shirt under a blazer. She approaches him from behind, walking stealthily, even though no one can see her anyway. She reaches out, grabs his right butt cheek, and gives it a little twist. He jumps and spins around. She laughs. He looks right at her with his piercing blue eyes. Smiling, she proceeds to run her hands over his chest before reaching up to kiss him on the lips. The next thing she knows, he dashes off. Ella smiled as she folded the mantra and slipped it into her desk. Let's see if he feels lonely now.

That night, she saw Milan, but only in a dream. He was wearing one of those white martial arts outfits. *It's called a gi,* a sweet voice whispered in her ear. *And see that belt? Black means he really knows what he's doing.* Ella whipped around to see who was speaking, but saw no one. When she turned back toward Milan, he was standing in a darkroom. He was wearing snug jean and the muscles of his arms rippled as he hung photos on a line. Ella squinted and saw they were all of her. *He knows who you are,* the voice whispered, *but do you know him?*

She sat up straight in bed, panting lightly, her face damp.

"Ella? Are you okay?"

She was about to say yes, but John had already rolled over to face the other way.

*April 14, 2012*

Ella: I was wondering ... do you believe in angels?

Milan: I kind of thought YOU were my angel.

Ella frowned. It had been a serious question, and he sidestepped it like he had so many others. How could she dream of a future with a man she barely knew?

Ella: I would like it very much if you would tell me more about yourself. I know you work a lot, and that you are always traveling, but what do you enjoy? What are your passions?

Milan: What do you wish to know, my love? I know I do not talk too much of myself, but I do share with you everything that is important: how I love my family, how I love you, how I felt when I lost my fiancée. But perhaps you want to know the "normal" things—that I enjoy photography and know quite a bit about it? Yes, I learned this from Ioana—she was passionate about photography—the lighting, the angles, the framing ... even with digital photography, but I prefer the old ways. I like being in the darkroom, watching the pictures come to life.

Ella shivered. Her dream! Milan had been in a darkroom ... and what about the voice? Who was that, whispering in her ear? She was about to reply when she heard a half-hearted knock, then John pushed the door open.

"Ella, we need to talk."

John left ten minutes later. Ella took a few slow, deep breaths, then, wiping the tears from her eyes, she read the new message Milan had sent.

Milan: What else...? When I was younger I studied martial arts. I did this as exercise, but since I often travel alone I like knowing that I can defend myself, if need be.

Oh! And I learn very quickly in "my sleep." The knowledge seems to come from nowhere, like understanding almost any language without trying to learn it.

And speaking of sleep, my love, I need some now. I don't know what is going on with me, but I feel very tired. Perhaps I am picking up on you. Why are you so sad? What do you really want? Good night, my love … and sweet dreams. Love, M<3

Ella put her head in her hands and began crying in earnest. A man she'd never met read her emotions from thousands of miles away, and her husband of nearly two decades didn't have a clue as to whom she really was.

*April 15, 2012*

Ella: You wrote that exactly when I felt you last night. Your timing couldn't have been better. Last night John came to my office while you and I were online. He knows things aren't right, and that I'm unhappy … but he has no idea why. I know he doesn't suspect … Anyway, he just stood there for a minute, quiet, then he said, "I love you"—which he never says—and that if I want to get separated or a divorce or marriage counseling … or whatever … he will. I mean, he didn't even seem to care which option I chose! I was so shocked I couldn't even say anything, although I knew what I wanted to say. Finally, he left.

Ella's chest felt tight as she hit the send button. Milan had asked what was wrong, but how would he deal with her reply? A few hours later, she had her answer.

Milan: Hello, my love. Over the last couple days, I have tried to "see" your husband again. He is definitely too American for my taste, but I like him. I know he loves you and always will, even if he doesn't know how to show it. Yeah, it's pretty hard for me to say this, but it is the truth. You have two men who want to see you happy.

*April 16, 2012*

The next day, Ella awoke to find there was no message from him. She wasn't all that surprised, for it was the day of his open house—a huge party—and he probably hadn't had a moment to himself. Still, given her revelation about John's visit to her office, she was still plagued with anxiety. She decided that today she would keep it light.

Ella: Good morning. I missed you last night. I know you're busy, with all the people constantly coming by, but when you have some time, I'd love a description of your three kids, please? Love you, Ella.

Milan: Good morning, my love. Yes, I have constantly people coming by ... but I have time for myself when I need it. I hired some people to take care of these things, for food, entertainment, etc. I am the host, but I have my own space for important things, like writing you. :)

Today is my day for "old people" but with a young heart … now I have to go but I will write later about my kids. I love you, Milan.

His words seemed no different than any other email, but Ella sensed a strong undercurrent. Something had changed for him, and it scared her to death. She quickly typed out another message.

Ella: I know you are concerned, and I know why. . I promise I won't do anything about my marriage until you know what you really want.

*April 17, 2012*

Milan: I just found out that my brother-in-law's mother died. I must take care of this problem until my sister and her family will be here from Italy. Oh baby, I'm on the road, driving home from the airport but I stopped to say good morning and to say I love you before you go … because I don't know exactly when I will get home. All my love, Milan

Ella: I'm so sorry to hear about your brother-in-law's

mother. Was she ill or was it very sudden?

He did not reply.

*April 18, 2012*

He did not reply the next day either. It was the longest they had gone without communicating, and Ella felt her emotions twisting like an out of control tornado. She found it impossible to concentrate, even at work. She knew in that moment, that she would have given anything, anything at all, to hear from him. The thought, the realization of the control he had over her, was terrifying.

*April 19, 2012*

Milan: Hi my love. I know you have waited for a note for me, and for that, I am truly sorry. But tell me, do you expect me to be happy that you are considering leaving your husband? I feel like—how it you say in America—a piece of garbage? I don't want to ruin your marriage. You have asked me to tell you more about myself. Well, for me, a vow made means more than life.

Milan: You say you will wait until I know what I really want, but this is not the issue. I already know exactly what

I really want in this unfair life. I have "seen" and "felt" you enough to know that you are my dream woman, the woman of my life ... and I want you so badly. I want you to be mine. I want you for myself.... I want to give you all my love, and I would do anything for you ... but we cannot be selfish.

I cannot be happy if I hurt someone else. Despite what you think, Ella, your husband loves you, your children may be nearly grown, but they still need stability. There has been a storm in my mind and an avalanche in my heart, but I think I must be the unluckiest man ever.

With a start, Ella realized the storm she had been feeling was his. They were sharing emotions—sharing the avalanche—even when they were not in direct contact. She felt a strange sensation in her chest—a mix of ecstasy and terror—that she had never known before Milan.

She didn't know what the future held, but she certainly remembered the past. She knew she hadn't truly been happy in her marriage for quite some time—years, in fact— even before she met Milan. Any passion and romance they once shared had dwindled long ago under the weight of careers and kids, and that weight had begun to suffocate Ella as well. She had begun to feel invisible to John, but it had never been quite so apparent until she met Milan. He, who had never met her in person, made her feel like the most beautiful, important woman in the world. She too considered vows sacred, but over the cost of herself? She thought back to how she used to judge others who had affairs; now she laughed at her own naiveté. Now she was glad she had never met him in person, because she knew she would never have been able to resist him. Then she would truly be an adulterer.

Ella: I can slow down, and put any thoughts of the future out of my mind for now, if that is what you wish. I love you, but it just isn't that … I can FEEL you when you are half way around the world, your emotions, your thoughts, your touch … and you can't tell me that doesn't mean something very important, at least to me it does.

I know how busy you've been. I hope tomorrow to get a little of your time, but I understand if I don't. All my love and passion goes to you. Love, Manuela

*April 20, 2012*

Milan: Okay, Ella, if you really love me you will not break your vows. I would not be able to live with it. You need him, even if you don't know it, especially since I cannot be by your side when you need it the most.

Yesterday I ended my "real life" relationship with Jasmine. Jasmine is not her real name, but I will not get into that right now. I broke her heart, but I cannot be with her because I am in love with you. I felt it wrong to mislead her, and to keep her tied to me when she could find another man who loves her.

Ella stared at the screen, her mouth working as if she'd tasted something bitter. Why was he telling her this—to torture her? He could leave "Jasmine", he could have his freedom, yet he expected her to stay in her marital prison. Suddenly she felt like she didn't know him at all. She was still fuming when she drifted off to sleep.

*Every inch of the ballroom was decorated. Live trees lined the wall, each strung with tiny white lights. Ella looked around, taking in the dance floor, the balloons, and the soft glow of the chandeliers. There was a small table set for the two of them; it was near a glass door with a view of the backyard—Milan's backyard. This was his home in Romania, and it was a mansion.*

*The room was filled with beautiful men and women, all in formal haute couture. Ella looked down at the gown she was wearing—it was a fine silk of deep purple, with a sparkly bodice that caught the light like tiny fires. A bell rang, signifying to the guests that it was time to be seated for dinner. There was a delicious lobster bisque for the first course, followed by grilled salmon. "Are you serious?" Ella said, laughing between sips of chilled champagne, "Fresh salmon in Romania? How did you get that?"*

*Milan gestured around the room, at all the beautiful people, and whispered, "Surely you know this is all for you, my love." After dinner, he swept her up in dance. Leonard Cohen's song "Dance Me to the End of Love" was playing in the background.*

*It was time for dessert, but they never made it back to the table.* Milan placed a hand on her arm and gently steered her toward a door partially hidden by one of the trees. It led to a narrow spiral staircase, which descended into Milan's private den. It was small and cozy, dominated by a large oak desk. There were tons of books and a fire burning in the fireplace. There was a knock on the door; then, at the sound of Milan's voice, a servant came with two bowls of homemade ginger ice cream, each topped with a cherry. There was a little chocolate gravy boat with fudge sauce, to add as desired.

Ella laughed as Milan demonstrated his skill at tying the cherry stem with his tongue, then raised an eyebrow to let him know that she was well aware of his prowess in that area. She vowed to buy a jar of cherries so she could practice, "Since I know how important vows are to you."

Then he pulled her into an embrace and they began to dance, slowly and without music, each moving the rhythm of the other. Then he gently pulled her down onto the plush rug in front of the fire. Eyes closed, Ella felt his lips press against hers, then onto her neck. He undressed her slowly, and she languished in the heat of the fire on her skin. Telling her to roll over, he began kissing her back. It was getting hotter, but now it had nothing to do with the flames. He kissed her shoulders, then down her back; showing off more of those tongue skills. She felt his body moving, hovering over hers, then he stood. At Ella's quizzical look, he said, "Turn over," and stepped back over to the desert tray. A moment later he returned with ice cubes, champagne and the little container of fudge sauce.

*Milan poured some of the champagne on her breasts and began to lick it off. Ella laughed as he poured the fudge down his own chest. "I know how much you love chocolate, my love."*

*From upstairs, they could hear the crowd counting down. "Three, two, one, Happy—"*

With a gasp, Ella sat straight up bed, and raised a shaking hand to pull the drenched nightgown from her body. This time it wasn't sex with Milan that had made her sweat; although that had certainly been hot. It was the fact that this encounter had taken place on New Year's Eve. For the first time ever, they had met in the future.

# CHAPTER SEVEN

*April 23, 2012*

Milan: Good morning baby. I've been sitting here, trying to write something but I can't find my words today. I have read and re-read everything you've written, trying to make sense of all of it, but all I get is just a headache. I would like to "see" and "feel" you happy, but … maybe later will be better. Just one thing, don't say you love me if you don't mean it.

Ella read his note and felt an ache begin over the bridge of her nose. If anyone understood the pain of trying to fathom the unfathomable, it was she. As she typed her reply she knew she was being flip, but she had nothing else to offer him right now.

Ella: Oh, Milan, don't think so much! Do you know what helps me when I can't think or have problems? Dancing.

She skimmed through her inbox and tried to compose an email to Shelby, but her mind was a million miles away. She finally settled for a generic, *let's together soon,* and signed off. Sometimes cleaning cleared her mind, so she went downstairs and got out the Swiffer. By the time she finished the kitchen floor and moved to the bedrooms, she was feeling better. She was bending down to pick up one of the boys' dirty shirts when a sudden chill ran along her spine, making her stop short. She stood straight up, looking around for someone. She was alone in the house, but she felt a presence … *his* presence. When she faced forward again, he was standing in front of her, his hand extended in invitation. She felt the beat of a Latin rhythm, the sound of a violin playing in the background. When he took her left hand and placed it on his right shoulder, she was shocked to find that he felt solid to the touch. Then he took her right hand into his left one. Her hand shot up in the air of its own volition, and then she could feel the warmth of his palm against hers.

He pulled her close, and she could feel the pressure of his hips close to hers. He started moving gracefully forward and Ella took several dance steps backward. Thank God no one was home, she thought, for if anyone walked in the room right now they would cart her away. She was wide awake and difficult as it was to believe, she couldn't deny the amazing sensation of dancing with him, the feel of him, in the flesh and in her home.

He certainly knew how to lead; she had never done this dance before but they moved together in perfect synchronicity. The music got stronger and she laughed out loud when he surprised her with a dip. They moved sideways, forward and back, with him guiding every step. He twirled her out, and brought her back in, and Ella felt like she was floating.

She looked into his eyes and saw the hunger in them. Holding her gaze, he seductively kissed her arm; then he brought his free hand under her nightgown. Suddenly, it was over; the energy was gone, replaced by a chill in the air. He had vanished. Ella stood there for a few minutes; when he didn't return, she sighed and went to get ready for work.

It was a struggle to concentrate on her patients that morning. She kept replaying their dance in her mind, and was still able to felt the warmth of his body against hers. Did this mean their connection was getting stronger, a future together more possible? Or was the Universe just messing with her? The answer seemed to change every time she thought about it.

As soon as she had a moment, she slipped into the doctors' lounge and pulled out her phone.

Ella: Our dancing was so much fun!! What was that?

Milan: That, my dear, was the tango.

Ella: Tango! Of course! I should have known, except I've never danced the tango before. But yes, the arm positions, the rhythm, and the seductiveness of it—it was wonderful. Especially with such an excellent instructor. :)

Milan: It's easy when one has such a beautiful and willing student. :)

Ella: But how did you do it? How was I able to feel you, physically?

Milan: I honestly don't know. I was thinking about you ... and suddenly there I was.

Ella looked down at the phone for a moment. Was that true? How could it be true? She decided not to push it, because she didn't know if she was ready for the answer.

Ella: Well, it was wonderful, and I hope the rest of your day was wonderful too. Teaching? At the university? Computer science? What did you say you are doing now? I LOVE YOU! Ella! <3

She spent the next few minutes waiting for a reply. It seemed like that was all she did these days—wait for a reply from him. It didn't come, and she slipped the phone back in her pocket, wondering why she suddenly felt like crying.

*April 24, 2012*

Milan: Good morning, my love. I'm sorry I didn't write you earlier, but I had to put out several fires at work, and a lousy Internet connection didn't help.

Ella: I understand....

Milan: Are you sure? Maybe I don't understand anything that's going on between us ... but I do know it will not be easy for us. I assumed this risk when I started to think that maybe we could have a future together. I don't know how, when or whatever, but I am a very patient man, with the head on my shoulders, and I've decided to wait and see what time will bring us. But this I know—I want all or nothing. That's why I will not come to you in "real life", not yet.

Ella stared at the screen, unsure of how to respond. She knew he was right—all or nothing was the only way it could work. She could not be married to John and carry on an affair—a real affair—with another man. *But this is a real affair, that guilty part of her said. You can call it whatever you want, Manuela, but you are cheating.* A second later, her computer beeped with a new message, and she pushed the thought to the back of her head.

Milan: Ufff ... sometimes I think I understand you ... but then you make me dizzy. You are sexy, funny, and smart, but if you have to say something, just say it or ask me whatever you want. If you are frustrated and pissed off, just know that the same thing is happening to me. If you want me to stay away, I will honor that as well.

Ella: I do not want you to "stay away" and I do not want

you showing up in real life either. I like what we have right now—I like it a lot—and I would be sad if you chose not to do this anymore. You seem to benefit less than I do, and I would have to accept it if you did stop.

I just don't understand how this can be. I've never heard of what we have been doing even existing before, and I've heard a lot of stuff. I've always believed that some people have psychic abilities, and I believe in other paranormal phenomena. But this? I can truly say that I was looking for a little harmless flirtation and romance, but perhaps I should have read a romance novel instead. So, yes, I do get frustrated and even a bit pissed off.

Would I like to be with you in real life? I believe so. But the idea of hurting the people I love ... I don't know if I could, even if you did offer to come here. I don't know a lot of things at this point. For now, I want to keep talking to you, if you are willing, because I love you, and it would seem our souls and bodies are connected as well as our hearts. I accept that only time will determine the outcome, and I will let it unfold as it is supposed to. I love you. Is that better? Ella

Milan: Yeah, it is better, and I just want you to know that I am in the same boat, as you Americans like to say. As long as we are honest about our feelings, things will play out as they should. Until then, we will keep busy with work and visit each other in spirit. And we will be honest. We are, as you say, connected, so there is no point in trying to hide our feelings from each other. I love you.

*April 25, 2012*

The next morning, Ella awoke feeling better than she had in a long time, and there was no doubt as to the reason why. She had an appointment with a psychic later that day, and just the prospect of gaining clarity about her relationship with Milan had eased the burden she had been carrying around. She was tired of trying to figure it out, worrying that he would misread her intentions, or that he didn't really care as strongly about her as he claimed. Even worse, she was tired of having an emotion and not knowing whether it was really hers, or if she was picking it up from him.

She was in the middle of a stretch when the night before came flooding back to her. She had been with him again, and it been one of the best nights yet. She felt as though she would never stop craving him. Then a memory flashed through her mind that made her actually laugh out loud. She grabbed her cell phone from the night table and dashed off a quick email.

Ella: I'm in a hurry, but I wanted to tell you quickly—that the little matchbox car you are looking for is under the ottoman in your living room. I saw it when we were there last night.

She went into the bathroom and turned on the shower, then began pinning up her hair so it wouldn't get wet. She caught her reflection in the mirror, startled by what she saw. It was as if she was seeing herself through Milan's eyes—still young, still sexy. John hadn't seen her that way in so long, maybe he never had.

When the mirror began to steam up, she went over and stuck her hand under the water to check the temperature. Just about right. She slid out of her nightgown and was about to step in when she remembered her phone, still lying on the nightstand. As she went back into the room to grab it, she tried to convince herself that she didn't want to miss any calls from work.

She stepped under the hot spray, hoping the water would wash away the mind chatter. It was important that she go to the psychic with a clear head; she would be easier to read that way. Just as she was drying off, the phone beeped.

Milan: Oh girl, you are really lucky that you're so far away.

I do have an ottoman, and the funny part is that I tried to find today that matchbox car. I thought the kids took them all home. Then my sister called to say a special one was missing from my nephew's collection. After I got your email I went and checked—and you were right! It was under the ottoman.

I love you, and I love that you were here. Now I am looking around, wondering where you are, my love.

Ella was about to write him back when she saw how late it was getting. She typed a quick xoxo, then finished getting ready. The psychic, a woman named Loreen, had an office in downtown Seattle, and Ella hoped the traffic wouldn't be too bad. On the way over, she reminded herself to reveal nothing and answer questions vaguely. She'd let Loreen do all the talking; it's the only way to know whether she was gifted or not. Even with some rubberneckers slowing past a fender bender, she arrived for her appointment exactly on time.

She pulled up to a small house; really, it looked like more of a cabin, with a low roof and dark brown shingles.

Ella pulled into the driveway, and saying a quick prayer that this woman was the real deal, turned off the ignition and got out.

The door opened before she even rang the bell. The woman was in her early sixties with gray, shoulder length hair worn in a bob. Her skin was weathered. She had hazel eyes, and a tired but friendly smile. The lines on her face suggested she had had a rough life. She was dressed in a threadbare but clean housedress, the kind Ella's grandmother had worn.

"Manuela?"

Ella smiled. "Yes, that's me."

"I'm Loreen. Please, come right in and make yourself comfortable." She gestured to one of two equally worn armchairs, separated by a low table.

Loreen waited for her to get settled in one, then sat down on the other. "I will need something of yours to hold during the reading. It needs to be something that you and only you wear or hold every day. Your watch or keys would work. I get my impressions based on the energy held in the item."

Ella nodded, then took off her watch and handed it to the woman. Loreen closed her eyes and took several slow deep breaths as Ella waited expectantly.

"You have questions," Loreen said quietly, then opened her eyes and stared straight into Ella's. "Your life is in turmoil right now."

Ella had to stop herself from rolling her eyes. Loreen had made a pretty vague statement, to say the least. But to be polite, she just smiled and nodded her head.

"You work in a service field, helping others," Loreen continued.

Another vague statement, another nod from Ella.

"You are troubled by a man … perhaps you should tell me a little about what is going on," Loreen said.

Of course she thought, but then whatever you say won't have as much value. Ella sighed and shifted in her seat, trying to hide her disappointment. "It is pretty complicated, but I'll try.

"I met a man online, and at first it was just flirting. Then, I started to dream about him, only the dreams felt so real. I could actually feel him touching me. I feel his feelings now, and sometimes his thoughts … and it is driving me crazy."

Loreen cast her eyes upward and took a few more deep breaths. "This man … he is deceiving you," she said in a faraway voice.

"*How* is he deceiving me?" asked Ella.

"I don't know, but I just keep hearing my guide say the word 'deception' over and over."

"He says he loves me," Ella whispered. It suddenly seemed so easy to believe the worst.

"He may even be dangerous," Loreen continued, "You need to stop all communication with him immediately."

"That is going to be pretty hard. I hear his voice in my head. I see his face, I can touch his body, and he can touch mine. I don't know how or why. I don't know how it started and I don't know how to make it stop," Ella said softly.

Loreen rubbed Ella's watch between two fingers. "I want you to stop talking to him on the Internet. Try it for two weeks straight."

Ella felt the tears coming. "I don't know if I can. I'm in love with him. I'm head over heels in love with him. I think about him constantly. He makes me happy. I love him."

Loreen shook her head. "I am telling you, this man is deceiving you."

"But *how* is he deceiving me? Does he not really love me like he says? Or is it something else?"

"He isn't who he says he is," the psychic kept on. "This sounds like something similar that I experienced. It has to do with astral projections. It is in my book. You should buy my book, you'll see! I wrote about this sort of thing."

Ella raised an eyebrow at Loreen's shameless advertising. Loreen took it as a question about astral projection.

"That's when your spirit leaves your body, it can go places and see things in another dimension. It is like flying, and your spirit is tied to your body by a silver cord so you can go back to it."

Ella nodded. "I have done some reading on this. I thought our telepathy for each other meant something like we were soul mates. I've never had this happen before, and I don't see a silver cord," Ella said.

"Soul mates? Ha!" she laughed. "No! He isn't your soul mate! You could do this with all sorts of people. This entire thing only means that you have some psychic abilities that you weren't aware of before. He could be some kind of a predator."

"I don't want to do this with all sorts of people!" Ella cried out, "I love him, and I'm only interested in doing this with him."

Loreen just slowly shook her head, like Ella was a stupid child.

"Just tell him you aren't going to talk for two weeks. If he really loves you, he'll be there when you get back. Love is patient."

"Okay," Ella agreed unenthusiastically, then asked Loreen the title of her book, if only to know which one to avoid.

Loreen wrote it down on a business card and handed it to Ella, along with her watch. "Let me know what happens."

Driving home, Ella just didn't feel right about the reading. She didn't think Loreen was all that great of a psychic. In fact, it occurred to her that Loreen was mixing up the two men that Ella talked to on her game. There was Milan aka SINGUR, but there was also that complete stranger, Hero. She had no feelings for Hero, and understood that his love was only pretend as well. Loreen could have mixed the two up. Well, it would be easy not to talk to Hero anymore, because she had already deleted her character. Maybe that's all there was to it.

She just couldn't help feeling disappointed that Loreen hadn't picked up on the thing that made their relationship so special. Whenever they were together, it had an ethereal feel to it, like she was completely enshrouded in love. She could feel his feelings—whether he was happy, sad, horny, frustrated, the whole works.

In fact, she smiled to herself, what made their relationship really great (and at times, really bad), was that if they were both happy, she was higher than a kite. It was as if their emotions compounded each other, and if they were both feeling passionate, it was like someone had slipped her a major aphrodisiac. If they were both sad, she was distraught. Everything was felt much more keenly. The highs were higher and the lows were lower with him. The best part was that she experienced his orgasms, too. He probably experienced hers, as well. The chemicals that are released in the brain when he came, or she did, were awesome, but when they both did … she was addicted. He made her high on sex.

It was like she had this special meter on him and him alone; so if he tried to lie to her, she would feel the deception too, right? All she had felt from Milan was passion, love, desire, and, lately, self-contempt.

After returning home, Ella debated with herself for about five seconds, then got on her computer to write Milan. She would tell him what Loreen had said, she decided, but she would keep it light.

Ella: Well, I went to the psychic. I don't think it was all that helpful. She said our telepathy has something to do with astral projections. She also said you could be dangerous, and that I should stop talking to you for two weeks, like that's going to happen, lol.

It was a few hours before he responded. Ella was making dinner and listening to her sons banter about the latest X-Box game and so-and-so's Facebook status when her phone buzzed. She pulled it out of her pocket and smiled when she saw it was from Milan. But the smile froze on her face when she saw what he had written.

Milan: Dangerous—what is that supposed to mean? Do you have any idea how I am feeling right now? Sorry baby, but I don't have time for games. If you want to play with this, you are free, but I will try to go on with my life and take care of my business ... and maybe I will say to you to get out of my life and leave me alone for good.

"Mom, are you okay? Mom! You look like you're going to cry."

Ella jerked her head up to find her sons staring at her.

"Oh—yes, I'm fine," she said, trying to control her voice, "I just got some bad news about a patient."

She hated to lie to her kids, but it wasn't like she could tell them that some spirit lover from across the world had just written her a Dear Jane email.

They looked at her a moment longer, debating whether they wanted to know more about the patient. Finally, they mumbled, "Sorry, Mom," and went back to their conversation. Ella turned her back on them, clicked reply on her phone, and began typing furiously.

Ella: Did you just say goodbye to me? I was just relaying what she said, not that I believed her.
I thought I could tell you anything. Yes, I do have a very good idea of how you are feeling ... because everything she said to me could have been equally said to you about me, and I know I'm not dangerous. I hope you change your mind. Love you still, Ella

He didn't reply that night or all the next day. Ella wrote him several little notes, trying to get a reaction.

Ella: What was that you said about a final decision? Love, Ella

Ella: I wasn't joking about anything at all. I'm trying to win you back here ... and I am failing. I love you, Ella

On the third morning, Ella woke up with a splitting headache, no doubt a result of crying herself to sleep. Her heart stopped when she looked at her phone and saw that he had written.

Milan: Sweetheart, I want to believe that our love is real and that this something very special, but I don't like this situation at all. I can't understand how this thing works and now I don't even want to understand it.

I only played that stupid game because that friend of mine wanted me to. For sure I wasn't looking for anything, but you found me and everything was changed and turned upside down. This astral projection or whatever it is … really freaked me out and scares me to death!

Yes, I can see that both of us are in the same situation. Maybe it's better to stay away for a while, without communication and without anything else, until we figure out what is going on. Two weeks, she said? Let's try it!

Ella felt her stomach lurch.

Ella: Do we have to try it right this second? Couldn't we try it in a couple of days from now?

Milan: The sooner the better, right? So, I will not be here and I will be nowhere. Even if this happens, that you feel me, please try to block me out. But for me, I think the best solution is to remind me—and yourself—that you are married. Milan

Ella didn't even respond. Instead, she went on Amazon and ordered Loreen's book. If they were going to follow this woman's advice, the least they could do is find out what else she had to say. She downloaded the book to her Kindle, then took the device to the couch in her office and curled up to read. A few hours later, she had finished it. She couldn't find any similarities at all between her story and the psychic's experiences. She felt duped; the woman had just wanted to sell a book, and perhaps drive a wedge between her and Milan. That part, she had certainly achieved.

*April 28–May 2, 2012*

They weren't on the game and they weren't emailing, but Ella could still feel Milan. He was sad and frustrated and angry and agonizing over the situation, just like she was. Once, around 1 a.m., he woke her and made love to her off and on throughout the night. There was no "talking" as they usually did, but there were still plenty of feelings of love and angst and desire coming through. She couldn't bear to do what he had asked, to block him out. She was so happy he was there. Then he would be gone again, and without a word.

She had agreed to this separation with no thought to his work schedule. So she had to laugh when she found herself making love to him in his classroom. Thankfully, no students were present at the time.

She kept telling herself, it's only two weeks, right? What is two weeks? Apparently, when you are passionately in love, two weeks is an eternity.

*May 3, 2012*

After nearly one week of no emails, Ella was going nuts. She created a new character and went on the game to look around. His character was still there, but apparently, SINGUR and Jasmine had game divorced. He also had a general message up that said he just wanted to be left alone. Well, she thought, she had been leaving him alone, oh … except between 2:00 and 5:00 a.m. that morning.

She knew she owed it to her game husband, Theo76, to let him know what was going on. So she signed back on as HealingGrace and gave him a brief synopsis of what was happening. Like any good friend, Theo76 wisely kept his advice to a minimal. He was surprised to learn that the man she was "in love with" was basically the same age he was, and after some encouragement from Ella, he admitted that he didn't think she should trust him.

After saying goodbye to Theo 76, she sent a message to SINGUR, his virtual do-not-disturb sign be damned.

Ella: Signed in and saw you were on. I thought you were going to pause from the game for two weeks, but I'm glad you didn't.

He answered right away, sending Ella's heart racing.

SINGUR: Relationships benefit from communication. I miss you.

Ella: I miss you too. Can things please go back to "normal" now, or at least our normal, LOL? I think it would be better to "talk" about our issues than try to ignore each other. I love you, Ella

Milan: My love, when I see your happy face, I don't need anything else! Yes, I know that talking about our problems is much easier and better than ignoring them. We're adults and we know our weaknesses and our limitations, trying to do all the best for us and the people we love. I love you so much, Milan

Overjoyed that they were writing again, Ella decided she wanted to do something special for Milan. She projected herself to his place. He wasn't home yet, and while she was waiting, she put on a sexy lingerie outfit—the bra, panties, garter belt, stockings and heels, all in black. He had never said anything, but she knew it was his favorite color.

She walked around his house a little bit, looking at things. He was a tidy man, but not obsessive-compulsive about it; she liked that.

Downstairs from the entryway was the large sunken living room with the stone-embellished fireplace; to the right of the entry was his office. Next to that was a wardrobe room larger than Ella's entire master bedroom. This man apparently liked his clothes very much. In the center of the room was an island of cedar and mahogany, which she supposed was a dresser. She didn't go snooping, but she expected that if she did she'd find his underwear or tee shirts inside. Instead, she looked around the rest of the room, noting the many pairs of fine shoes lined up on the floor, and the shirts and other items hanging on the walls.

Going back to the living room, she looked out the glass

doors, the ones they had their "New Year's Eve" dinner by. The pool in the backyard was covered, and there was a Jacuzzi nearby, which was also covered.

She walked back to the kitchen, trying to think of something she could surprise him with. She opened all the cabinets, not finding much to choose from. Clearly he ate out a lot, but with whom? She opened the fridge and pulled out a bottle of chocolate sauce with French writing on the label, then went back to the cabinet where she had seen a saucepan. She put it on the stove and turned the heat on low.

She had poured the chocolate in the saucepan and was stirring it when she heard the door open. A moment later, Milan walked into the kitchen. He stopped there near the kitchen table, and froze. His jaw dropped, and he blinked his gorgeous blue eyes a couple of times. Then he collected himself, smiled, and walked towards her. He placed one hand behind her back, the other behind her head, and gave her a long kiss hello. She moved her hand to the front of his pants and could feel his desire hardening there.

Ella re-entered her body with such force that she felt like the wind had been knocked out of her. She was back home, sitting in front of her computer. She glanced at the clock and saw that only a few minutes had passed. It felt like much longer.

Ella: Milan, my sweet love. How is everything going with you?

Milan: Oh baby, I think you know how everything is

going! Imagine my surprise when I went into the kitchen, looking for coffee as usual, and found you there instead. Standing in front of me with your big brown eyes, full of desire. I could feel your kisses and your touch on my body, but then suddenly you were gone. I couldn't figure out exactly what had happened.

Ella: I know! I wonder what interrupted us! Oh well, there is always next time. Love, M<3

Milan: I'm sorry; I don't have time to write much, but this song is for you:

Song: "I'd Love You To Want Me" by Lobo.

Ella: Thank you for the song, Milan. And please don't feel pressured to talk to me. I understand how demanding work can be, or that you might need space. When you are ready and have time, I'll be here. Take as many days as you need. Love, Ella


*May 4, 2012*


Milan: Ella, my love. I sit down to write you, but more and more lately I can't find the words or I tend to lose my thoughts. Anyway, I just wanted to wish you a good morning and a day as wonderful as you are. All my love, Milan

Ella: I know what you mean. I'm having trouble sleeping … and I miss you and I want you so much. But I've been thinking a lot about this—especially when we weren't writing—and I believe we must be soul mates. There are over a million different ways to love, unique to each relationship. I love my husband. I love you. I love both my sons equally, but in different ways too. I admire certain things about each one of them, and they are different things. I love my husband, because he has always been my friend, but over the past few years I haven't felt connected to him. He doesn't make me feel good about myself, so I don't desire intimacy with him.

How can that be, completely disconnected from the man sleeping next to me—who I have children with—and so in sync with you, a man on the other side of the world?

At the same time, we get something different from everyone. I thought I would get some clarity from that psychic, but you know how that went. Her book was no help either, but I've found another on soul mates that seems to hit it on the nose. Still, we are even more connected than what the author describes.

T he love I feel for you is so powerful that it overwhelms me. I've never felt this way before. I don't know much about reincarnation, but I'm starting to think that maybe we were lovers or even married in a past life or lives. The feelings that I have for you seem infinite, like I've known you since I the very moment I was born, or before that.

I think we are actually twin flames. Have you ever heard this term? Supposedly, they are one soul that God split into feminine and masculine components. Spiritualists speculate that we have about twenty soul mates that we encounter them in each life to work on problems; but there is only one twin flame.

Typically, the twin flame stays spirit bound while their other half is living in a body, but as the soul evolves, there will come a time when they are both in a physical body, living on this earthly plane. That book was very clear on one point—no marriage can survive if one of the marriage partners should encounter their twin flame. The attraction is too strong. They have to be together.

It also says though if for some reason twin flames cannot be together, Reiki can help them to heal.

It is hard to explain to someone that I don't need a picture of you, because I see you clearly every day. I don't need a phone call from you because I can already hear your voice.

Yet, I love your words. English isn't your first language, yet I think you speak more eloquently than any American I've ever met. I wish I understood more languages. Yet it doesn't seem to matter. I love the way Italian, French, and Romanian sound when those words roll off your tongue. I understand the meaning somehow on an instinctual basis, since I don't know the language.

What is happening between us is amazing! It has to mean something, it just has to.

I LOVE YOU, Manuela

Milan: I know how you feel, baby, and I feel the same. I don't know if I understand this twin flame stuff, but it certainly seems to fit our situation.

*May 5, 2012*

Over the past few days Ella had become more and more convinced that she and Milan were two halves of the same soul. On the one hand, she was ecstatic that they were communicating again; on the other, she could feel his pain, sadness and confusion. There were too many strange things for him, or many questions without answers, and it was wearing him down. Half the time Ella believed they might have a real future together, the other half she expected him to end it for good.

She was mentally drained herself, so much so that she was actually relieved to be going to the medical conference in Redondo Beach tomorrow. Usually she dreaded these things; she had to smile and kiss-kiss with doctors she hadn't seen since the previous conference, and she always returned to work to find a million things to catch up on. This time, though, it was just nice to get away. She had even rented a little convertible Mustang to drive while she was there. John had raised an eyebrow at this uncharacteristic move, but had said nothing. She knew she was doing all this in an effort to keep her mind off Milan; she also knew she was kidding herself.

Early the next morning, she dashed off a quick note to Milan, telling him about the conference. *These things are so boring*, she wrote, *so tell me about your hopes, your dreams.*

*Where would you like to visit?* She was going to write more, but then she heard John rattling around in the kitchen. A wave of guilt washed over her as she clicked the send button.

# CHAPTER EIGHT

*May 5, 2012*

The next morning, Ella awoke early feeling refreshed and full of energy, even though she had only slept a few hours. John was still asleep, something she was grateful for as she crept about the dark bedroom, grabbing the comfortable slacks, white blouse and scarf she would wear on the plane. She laid the clothes out on her side of the bed, smiling at the white cardigan she had bought in case the ride in the convertible was chilly. Then she grabbed a fresh towel out of the linen closet and slipped into the bathroom, careful to shut the door so the light wouldn't wake him.

As she stepped into the steaming shower, she tried not to think about how happy she was to get away from her husband for a few days. Well, maybe happy was too strong a word—-it was more like relieved. Lately it had become more and more difficult to be in the house with John. The distance that had been growing between them over the past few years had become separate lives. When the boys were around they'd make some small attempt at conversation, but as soon as they were alone they retreated to their own corners of the house. It seemed to Ella that they were counting the minutes until one could say to the other, "I'm running out to the store," or "I'm going for a run." Then Ella would feel this rush of relief, as if the air in the room was suddenly lighter. John had to feel it too. Had Milan caused this, or had it always been there and she was just noticing?

The day before had been one of the longest in recent memory. Ella spent the morning doing laundry and packing for the medical conference. She had just finished applying a pore minimizing masque when John announced his presence with a tap on the open bathroom door. The gesture was just one small example of the politeness that characterized their relationship.

"Hey," he said, smiling when he saw her face covered with thick white goop. "I'm heading out—got some things to take care of at the office."

*That was a new one.*

"Really? On a Saturday?"

Ella's tone was one of curiosity, not suspicion, so why did John suddenly avert his eyes?

"Yeah, just a few things. No big deal."

"Okay, well, I'll just be here, getting ready for my trip." She turned back to the mirror. "Pizza okay for dinner? The boys will be home."

"Sure, Ella. See you later."

She heard his footsteps fading down the hall and sighed. How much longer could they live like this? No matter how

John acted, he couldn't be happy. He deserved more; they both did.

The following morning, she was still thinking about this as she finished dressing and slipped her feet into a pair of loafers. She looked down at her husband, asleep in the bed they had shared for over a decade, wondering if she should wake him to say goodbye. *Let him sleep,* she told herself, knowing it was a cop-out. A few minutes later she placed a hastily scribbled note on the pillow next to him. Then she grabbed her suitcase and headed out to the driveway, where the taxi was waiting to take her to the airport.

It was only a two-and-a-half hour flight from Seattle to Long Beach, but as Ella fastened her seat belt for takeoff, the time stretched out like an eternity. She spent thirty minutes tapping her foot on the floor before she figured out why she was so restless—she wasn't used to sitting *anywhere* for more than fifteen minutes at a time. Even when she was supposedly "relaxing", her mind was on overdrive, thinking about work or kids or ... *who are you kidding, Ella?* For the past several months, all of her mental energy had been spent on Milan, and little else.

Determined to savor her few days away from home, she closed her eyes, took a few deep breaths, and tried to quiet her mind. The woman next to her mistook her behavior for a fear of flying and asked if she was okay. The two struck up a conversation that lasted until they touched down in California. Her attempt at meditation had been thwarted, but Ella didn't mind. Other than her patients, it wasn't often that she got to chat with someone new; besides, it was a few hours she wasn't able to dwell on Milan.

Her mood improved even more when she saw her rental car, a red Mustang GT with the top already down. She could barely keep the smile from her face as the guy from Hertz placed her bag in the back seat and handed her the keys. As she pulled away, she could almost pretend that she could skip the conference, keep driving, and be free of it all. She pretended this even as got on the I-405 northbound and headed for Redondo Beach.

The phone dinged with a message just as Ella was pulling into the parking lot of her hotel. Already exhilarated from driving with the wind in her hair, she now felt that familiar quickening in her pulse, that hope that it was a reply from Milan. As she pulled up to the valet she glanced at the phone and saw that it was indeed from him; but, wanting to prolong the anticipation, she decided she'd wait to read the message until after she had checked in. A few minutes later, after the porter let her into her room, she pulled out her phone.

Milan: Ella, my love, it is Saturday night and I'm home, doing nothing. Tomorrow I plan to devote the whole day to my mother, to take her somewhere she likes and do whatever she wants. But tonight I wanted to be alone and write you.

My future plans? The future is a big place, dear Ella. Right now, I just want to breathe a little … but this next month is going to be to very busy at the university where I'm working now, and of course I want to be here next month so I can spend my nephew's birthday—and mine—with my family. After that, I have to continue my work in Europa ... and who knows where else?

I hope to visit China someday and another dream of mine is to go to Brazil. Goals that I want to achieve...? Yeah, I have some. You know already about my work with orphans and other disadvantaged children, but another project I have in my head and hope to achieve someday is a place for the elderly who have no family and nowhere to go. I want to build a place that feels like home and says thank you for all they contributed in life. This is a very old dream of mine, from when I was little more than a boy.

The rest of his message rambled on about how for the first time ever he had slept for eight hours and that this was surely Ella's influence, but Ella was no longer paying attention. She was too busy trying not to cry. She had asked him about his plans for the future and he had rattled off some places he wanted to see and an old age home he wanted to open. Lofty pursuits, but where did she fit into them? Did she fit at all? Ella felt all the excitement about her trip draining out of her. She typed a curt reply about how she had been sleeping less, then she placed her phone on silent, threw it in her purse, and sat down on the bed, completely deflated. She had been looking forward to a day of sun, sand, and freedom; now all she to look forward to was tomorrow's lectures on diabetes and hypertension.

She looked around the room, tempted to take a nap, when she noticed the sun streaming in through the window. *This is ridiculous—it's a gorgeous day and I'm in Redondo Beach. I'm not wasting it moping around a hotel room.* She walked over to her suitcase, glad that in addition to the usual boring slacks and conservative blouses she had packed a pair of khaki shorts and a pair of flip-flops. She quickly changed into them, then headed out for a walk on the boardwalk that ran along the shoreline. The salty air and the sound of the waves lifted her mood, and she had almost forgotten about Milan's message ... until she saw the small, quaint beach house with a sign out front: Psychic Readings by Staci. Ella paused for a moment, undeniably tempted to go in but afraid after her last reading. What if this Staci woman was just another fraud?

She started walking and was almost past the house when she admitted that her curiosity was stronger than her skepticism. *Maybe she's reading someone else. Maybe she's not even home....* But Ella only had to knock once, when a petite, pretty woman answered the door and ushered her in. She was around Ella's age and spoke with a Bulgarian accent. *It's probably not even a real accent,* Ella thought, figuring she had a right to her cynicism after all she had been through recently.

Smiling warmly, Staci led Ella into the small room where she did her readings. There were two wing chairs with a table in between them. On the table was a box of tissues, standard for every psychic and psychiatrist.

"You don't need to say anything," Staci said as they settled themselves into the chairs, "I will tell you everything."

*We'll see about that,* Ella thought, but she smiled and

nodded.

Staci stared intently at her for a long moment, then said, "Please close your right hand and make two wishes, but do not tell me what they are."

Ella did as she was told, folding her hand into a loose fist and thinking hard about what her wishes should be. It felt she had too many to just pick two. Finally she decided that her first wish was for a happy marriage—no matter whom it was with; the second wish was that if it *were* with Milan, she would know exactly how this marriage would come about. She lifted her head and nodded at Staci that she was ready.

Taking Ella's palm, Staci closed her eyes and inhaled deeply. "You will have a long healthy life," she began, "living to about ninety years old. You are very sensitive and you get hurt easily by people, especially those who talk about you behind your back. You have a family member you have not seen for a long time. This person will get in touch with you and you will be very surprised by this."

Ella had vowed not to react to anything Staci said. Still, at the mention of a long lost family member, she felt her hand clench. Could it be her birth mother? She looked up at the ceiling, but said nothing. Well, that would certainly be a surprise.

"Did you know that people's lives work in nine year cycles?" Staci asked, startling Ella from her thoughts. "You will be starting a new nine-year cycle soon, and this will be a good thing." She inhaled again, then added, "Yes, this next cycle will be a very happy one for you."

*Well, that's good to know,* Ella thought, *but what does*

*that really mean? There is no way for me to gauge whether it's accurate.*

"You have worked very hard your whole life, since you were thirteen years old. You have been let down and betrayed by many people. You have trouble trusting people now. There were people who should have helped you along, but failed to do so."

Ella gave her a half-nod, half-shrug; it was true to a certain extent. She *had* started working when she was thirteen years old, babysitting. But didn't a lot of people do that? Yet she had never stopped working from that time to when she started to medical school. She had always had a side job to help pay her own bills. This was different from many of her counterparts, who had the luxury of concentrating on their studies without worrying about the rent being paid. She never took vacations; she had always been all work, no play … *until Milan.*

"…and there was a major struggle and change at your work," Staci continued, "about nine years ago."

Ella nodded again, this time genuinely surprised. She remembered like it was yesterday the turmoil at the clinic. It had been discovered that some of the family practice doctors had negotiated much better salaries than the others. They were all doing the same job, but the pay structures weren't equitable. When this got out, some of the doctors left; many stayed, but there was a lot of hard feelings and distrust of the administration after that.

"You will be starting school again soon, but you are not to change careers. It is important you stay a medical doctor." Staci smiled.

She had scored with that one, and she knew it, too. Ella had to admit she was impressed; this lady was good. Then again, maybe she had seen her at the conference or knew doctors were in town for one. Still, it would have been a great guess; in her casual clothes and hair pulled back in a ponytail, Ella certainly wasn't dressed like a doctor. Not to mention the fact that most doctors didn't walk into a place and ask for a psychic reading.

"You will be presented with an opportunity; a shift in your work is coming. Again, they say it is important you stay in the medical profession."

"They," Ella knew, were the spirits who were talking to Staci.

"There are many uncertainties going on right now. The home you live in … it will change soon. You will be living in another house … maybe in a few months.…"

That comment made Ella's eyebrows rise up in surprise. She hadn't seen *that* coming.

Suddenly Staci's eyes locked onto hers, and Ella found it impossible to look away. "Do you love your husband?"

"Yes," Ella answered honestly. After all, Staci hadn't asked *in what way* she loved him. *Let's see what she says now.*

Staci sighed loudly. "You love him, yes, but you don't feel connected to him anymore … not for the past three years. The problem between the two of you has to do with how he was raised. There are family issues there. He loves you, though. He is also under a lot of stress at work right now."

*Stress at work?* John hadn't said anything to her about

it. For a moment Ella was angry that he had not confided in her, then she stopped, horrified. She had been keeping an entire life from him!

"There is another man. You speak to him with your heart chakra." A dreamy look came over Staci's face; it was almost as if she were in a trance. "This man is across the seas." She held her arm up and made a wave motion with her fingers.

Now Ella was looking at her, openly shocked. Clearly, Staci was getting some solid information from a very talkative spirit.

Staci smiled and gave her a knowing look. "You talk to this man through the computer, no? This man across the seas, you have not seen him? You are attracted to him, though?" She paused for a few seconds, and when Ella didn't answered, she said, "Yes, he is very attractive. 'Easy to look at', as they say."

That made Ella smile. Easy to look at—now that was an understatement if she ever heard one.

"You have a strong sexual connection to this man, but it's much more than that. I can see you in a happy marriage with *him*. He is your soul mate." Staci stopped to give Ella that unnerving stare again. "There are spiritual mates and there are soul mates. We can have many spiritual mates, but only one soul mate. Your current husband is one of those spiritual mates." Again she closed her eyes and inhaled deeply. "There was another spiritual mate, a long time ago and losing him changed everything for you. Was there a car accident?"

Ella nodded, feeling that awful sensation in pit of her

stomach. She got it whenever she thought about Jason. When he died she'd certainly felt like she lost her soul mate.

"Did you know that your female chakra is completely closed off?"

Ella shook her head and braced herself for the inevitable sales pitch. She had been to psychics who claimed to be able to remove curses and bring about spiritual healing ... all for the "low cost" of $300.

"Yes, your chakras are out of balance," Staci continued. "I suggest Reiki or some other kind of energy work." She gave Ella a pointed look; it was as if Staci knew of her suspicions. "I suggest you find a reputable practitioner where you live."

Pleasantly surprised, Ella smiled at her and nodded. "I will."

"Good. Now, I have more to tell you. Let's see, what religion are you?"

"Catholic," Ella replied.

"Do you accept that religious denomination does not matter, so much as accepting there is one God, one light, one universal spirit?"

"Yes," said Ella.

"Okay, good. It is important that you understand that God will not hurt another so you can be happy—it doesn't work that way. You understand this, right?"

Ella nodded yes.

"The man across the seas, he will come here, when he is ready. You are not to ask him to come, and under no circumstances are you to go there. This man, he has a woman in his life right now—"

Staci cut herself off when she saw the look on Ella's face. "He does *not* love this woman," she said, giving Ella's hand a gentle squeeze, "but he does feel some sort of obligation towards her. There was another woman that he did love very much, but she is now in the spirit world...."

Staci trailed off and her eyes seemed to roll back in her head. She looked so strange that for a moment Ella wondered whether her head was going to start spinning altogether. She knew Staci was talking about Ioana, the fiancée Milan had lost to the drunk driver.

"Yes, I know."

"...and ever since then, he has been searching, searching, searching.... You will be very happy with this man. There will be people gossiping, saying mean things about you. You should ignore them." A slow smile split Staci's face. "But the two of you will be very happy."

"But how...?" Ella began, "When—"

"You feel trapped, like a bird in a cage. This is temporary. Do not tell your husband about this man, just continue to communicate with him as you have been." She peered at Ella. "How many children do you have?"

"Two," Ella replied, feeling like Staci had certainly earned the right to ask a question. She was amazing.

"No miscarriages?"

"No."

"That is funny, I clearly see three children for you," Staci remarked.

Ella sighed. "No, just one pregnancy, twin boys, and no miscarriages. Three children, you say?"

Staci shrugged but said nothing else. Milan had said he'd hoped for children of his own. Maybe she wasn't too old after all. There were a lot of women having children in their forties these days.

"So is this what you truly want?" Staci asked. "Do you want to be together with the man from overseas?"

Even as Ella nodded, she saw the faces of John and the boys flash before her.

"Remember … you cannot hurt someone to obtain what you want. The universe doesn't work that way.…"

"Okay…," Ella said, confused. But if she was with Milan, she would hurt John, wouldn't she?"

As if reading her thoughts, Staci held up a hand. "Your husband … there is a woman he has noticed at work."

"Oh…," Ella said, swallowing her surprise. She remembered the day before, when John had gone to the office to "take care of a few things."

"She only recently started here. Your husband has not betrayed you, but he does admire this woman very much. He feels this rift between the two of you, and he has felt it for a long time."

Ella nodded. Of course he did, and no matter whose fault it was, she couldn't blame him for taking an interesting in someone else.

Staci paused to take another deep breath. By now Ella knew it meant she was getting more information and she waited patiently for her to speak.

"The ocean, and the water, they are very dear to your spirit. You are not 'at home' where you currently are living. Pay attention to your dreams, especially those with water in them. In the next thirty days a big change is going to occur. Be patient. I will pray for you, and I want you to write down your dreams and call me in a week. Oh, and Ella, I want you to promise me that you will not speak to any other psychics."

Ella thought that was a strange thing for her to say, but she nodded anyway. She wanted this relationship with Milan desperately, and she would have agreed to just about anything.

She fished the cash out of her purse and handed it to Staci, a bit surprised when the woman grabbed her in a tight hug. "Patience," she repeated, and handed Ella her business card.

Ella thanked her for the reading and left the house, debating what to do with the rest of her day. It was high tide, and the waves seemed to be calling her, so she took off her shoes and walked slowly along the sand, stopping every now and again to pick up a shell and mulling over every detail of the reading. It was late afternoon when she got back to the hotel, and as she walked to the elevator bank she realized the last thing she wanted to do was sit in her room all night. Then she remembered the convertible, just sitting there in the parking lot. With a new sense of purpose, she hurried to her room, changed back into her jeans, and rang for the valet to bring her car around.

An hour later, she was driving up the Pacific Coast Highway when she spotted an adorable Italian bistro right on the water. As if on cue, her stomach rumbled, and she realized she hadn't eaten since the buttered roll she'd had on the plane. Ella had never been one to dine alone, but the place was so lovely, and certainly preferable to going hungry. She asked for a table facing the water, then ordered the fresh catch of the day and a glass of Pinot Gris. As she sipped her wine, watching the sun go down on another day, she knew she was no closer to any answers. *Have patience,* she mumbled to herself. It seemed she had no other choice.

# CHAPTER NINE

*May 9, 2012*

For the next couple of days, Ella checked her phone as little as possible. Of course she still wanted to hear from Milan, but the reading with Staci had changed things for her. If they were meant to be together, it would happen, but in the right time and without hurting John's feelings. Pushing it or getting upset every time Milan sent her a noncommittal message would not make it happen any faster, or at all. It would just make it harder for Ella to live in her present reality. Still, she had to smile when she woke up the day after the conference and saw this message:

Milan: Good morning, my love. I know you are probably catching up on things after your doctor's conference. I just wanted to let you know that you have changed my life forever. We'll talk more later, but this song just popped into my head, and I wanted to share it with you. All my love, Milan.

Song: "If You're Not The One" by Daniel Bedingfield.

Before her reading with Staci, Ella would have spent the rest of the day trying to decipher what he meant by those particular words and why he had sent that particular song. Today, she just took a deep breath and said, "Patience." It had become her new mantra.

Ella: Thank you. That song expresses things so well. My heart says that we are made for each other, but I will understand if you want to give it a rest for a while. You know, try to busy ourselves with work and other things? I can't help but think of you constantly, but if that is what you want, I will try. Love, M<3

Milan: No, baby … I think I want to be surprised by time and go with the flow. I like to live in the moment, trying to enjoy it. In the end we will find a way to be happy and grateful for all that we have.

Ella smiled. It sounded like something Staci would say. It was a sign that if she really had patience, it would all work out in the end. That resolve sustained her for several days, until Milan simply disappeared.

*May 15, 2012*

She could not understand it. The week following the conference, it was the same seamless flow——with Milan and Ella exchanging love notes and little tidbits throughout the day, followed by their visits at night. Ella was getting less sleep and he was resting more—it was as if their bodies were syncing up, preparing them for the "real life" Staci had predicted. Then one day, he just stopped responding to her messages. She wanted to believe that he was just busy with work, but after the third day she had to admit it was something much more than that. She had gone to bed early that night hoping to "see" him, but all she had felt was waves of his pain, sadness and conflict. When he did think of Ella, it was almost in a clinical sense, a cold evaluation. Ella fought the urge to sob. Had he decided to be with Jasmine after all? He had said it was over and Staci said it was just an obligation, but maybe it was an obligation he wanted to live up to.

Finally, at 4:30 a.m., she rolled over, grabbed her phone from the nightstand, and typed him a message.

Ella: You are killing me here! ALL NIGHT LONG all I felt was your pain and sadness. And why haven't I heard from you? I don't understand what has changed. Please talk to me.

She pressed send, put the phone down, and fell into a deep, exhausted sleep. When she awoke, John was long gone and her eyes looked like she had been punched. She had been dreaming of the ocean, she realized, but she was too tired to remember it, let alone write it down as Staci had suggested. She knew even before she looked at the phone that he had not written back.

Ella: If you want me to leave you alone for a while, I will do that. I won't like it, but I can do it. When you're sad and angry, I feel it too, and it makes me feel the same way.

Ella: I don't even know if you are reading these messages, so I guess this will be the last one. My love for you hasn't changed, but I cannot keep pleading for answers you clearly do not want to give. I always knew … when you let go I would have to as well. Goodbye with love, Ella

And Ella did try to let him go. She tried from the minute she woke up in the morning to find her eyes were once again red and swollen. She tried as she did the housework and when she asked the boys what they wanted for dinner. Everything required Herculean effort, from lifting her toothbrush to telling yet another person that, yes, she was okay. When John asked her what was wrong she tried to pass off her haggard appearance as allergies.

The only place she found some refuge was at work, where she didn't have to face her family or her own questions as to what had happened. Several times she considered calling Staci, but she was too bitter to bother. If the woman gave her one more hopeful prediction, Ella would have fallen apart altogether.

May 25, 2012

Ella was just getting out of the shower when she heard her phone beep with a message. Thinking it was a reply from a colleague, she slipped into her robe and walked over to the nightstand. As she tapped the screen, her stomach dropped and her heart began to race. It was from Milan.

Milan: Ella, I know you must be very angry with me. I cannot explain it yet, but I have been going through something—am still going through something—that I must deal with alone. I cannot deny what I feel for you, but there are other things to consider, both on your side of the world and on my mine. My mind tells me to run ... my heart tells me to stay ... and I am sometimes torn between the two. But I am not running, and I'm so very sorry that I hurt you. Please forgive me.    At the bottom of the message, he had embedded a song:

"Maybe" by Enrique Iglesias.

Ella stared at the phone for a moment, fighting the urge to throw it across the room. That was the message she had waited for—begged for—for ten agonizing days? And to add insult to injury, he had sent her a song entitled "Maybe"! She took several deep breaths, trying to quell the unfamiliar feeling in her gut. As she placed the phone back on the nightstand, she realized what it was. Rage.

She didn't answer him all that day. She didn't know

what to write and she didn't want to say anything she would regret. Finally, just before going to bed, she went down to the computer and signed on.

Ella: Let's just cool it for a while. Take some space, work our own stuff out. I can only assume that this conflict has to do with Jasmine—what else couldn't you talk to me about, unless it was another woman? I love you to the very depths of my soul, but I cannot endure the silent treatment again. Ella

She clicked send, sat back in her chair and pressed her hands to her temples. It was the coldest she had ever been with him, but it had to be done. Patience was one thing; giving him all the control was another. It had never much bothered her, until she saw how much damage he could do with it. She placed her hand back on the mouse and was about to sign off when he replied.

Milan: Ella, this has nothing to do with Jasmine. My relationship with Jasmine is over. I made my choice. Yes, I still talk with her, but it is just a polite "hi" and "bye." I just needed to be alone for a while. I hope you can forgive me for this. All my love, Milan

Ella was more confused than ever, but she could not deny the relief she felt. Maybe Staci had been wrong, maybe he did not feel an obligation to Jasmine after all. Once again she thought about calling the psychic, but she just felt it would muddy things further. For now, she knew she had no choice but to forgive him and try to forget.

Around 4:15 a.m. the next morning she woke up to find herself in Milan's house. She didn't see him and knew he was at work. There was a suitcase open on the bed—her suitcase—and she was packing to leave; they were taking some time apart. She was about to leave him a note, but then decided to wait so they could say their goodbyes face to face.

An hour later, she heard his key in the door and braced herself, for a fight, a breakup—she didn't know. She already had her coat on and was standing in the hallway near the kitchen. Her suitcase was on the floor next to her. As Milan entered the front door, a fire magically appeared in the fireplace. Ella looked at it in surprise, then at Milan, wondering if he had a remote for it, but he just shrugged. Then he walked over, took her hand, and led her to the couch. They sat next to each other for a few moments, making awkward small talk, each waiting for the other shoe to drop. Then he turned to her and gently stroked her face with his hand.

Ella closed her eyes, enjoying his caress, and when she opened them she saw him looking at her with that glint of passion in his eye. Ella narrowed her own eyes, thinking, "Oh, no you don't … don't even think about it." But the next thing she knew, he was pulling off her coat....

Afterward, they lay on the floor, cuddling by the fire. "I'm sorry," Milan whispered, his breath warm against her neck. In reply, she turned over and began kissing him again, the last of her anger and resistance melting away.

Ella awoke with a start. She was in her own bed, and it

was 5:30 a.m. Next to her, John exhaled noisily and rolled over as if in protest. Utterly exhausted, she lay back against the pillow and closed her eyes.

*June 1, 2012*

Milan: Today I must go to Vienna for work. I will be very busy, but I should have time to spend with my favorite woman. Do you want to go with me? Love you, Milan

Ella smiled at the message. She was on her lunch break, munching on a salad and listening to some of their songs, which she had added to her iPod under the playlist, "Forever". Somehow, the songs always made her feel closer to him. Since the night they had "made up" their relationship had for the most part returned to normal—at least, *their* normal. She had even managed to "visit" him for his birthday on the 29th, showing up in his bedroom in a black teddy and thigh highs. Still, her curiosity about the reason for his disappearance lingered, and it had taken all of her strength not to pressure him about it.

Ella: I WOULD LOVE TO GO WITH YOU TO VIENNA! I want to travel everywhere with you. Any ideas about what a girl should pack, LOL?

A few hours later, he replied:

Milan: Hi baby, I just arrived at the hotel and it is perfect. I miss you and I'll "see" you soon. Don't worry about clothes; I have taken care of that. Love you, Milan

*June 2, 2012*

The next morning, Ella woke up just as John was getting ready for his run. She lay in bed, pretending to be asleep, unable to bear another polite conversation, especially after the night she had spent with Milan. She wasn't sure, but she thought she felt John standing over her, looking down as if he wanted to say something. Then she heard the creaking of the bedroom door as he pulled it shut behind him.

As soon as he was gone, she ran down to the computer. She couldn't wait another minute to find out if all she had seen last night was real. She opened up Google, typed in Vienna, and clicked on the first page that came up.

At first she found the usual standard facts: "Vienna is the capital of Austria, and its largest city. It is close to the borders of the Czech Republic, Slovakia and Hungary. It is often said to be 'The City of Dreams' because it was home to Professor Sigmund Freud."

Ella had to smile. *How was that for irony?*

She skimmed the rest of the page, finding more facts she already knew. "The city is famous for music and art. The primary language spoken is German. The city is known for its lavish ballrooms and there are several balls throughout the year."

When she reached the photographs of Austria, her heart began to race. *That is exactly what I saw!* she thought as she looked at the photographs of the Schonbrunn Palace. It was a magnificent structure of tan color that turned to shimmering golden yellow when touched by the sun. Surrounding the palace were beautiful gardens and an area where concerts were held. There was even a zoo.

She even found a photo of the café inside the Gloreitte Garden, where she and Milan had sat at a small table, holding hands as they sipped their coffees. Now, just staring at the picture, a tingle was running up her spine. To see evidence that they had been together in a real place was completely amazing to her.

Later, in their hotel, he'd had some Western outfits delivered to their room for them to wear out that evening. She looked at him questioningly, but he just laughed and told her to trust him. She put it on, marveling at its perfect fit; it was as if it had been made just for her. Milan looked so hot in jeans and a cowboy hat, she couldn't stop staring at him as they left the hotel and hopped into a cab. A few minutes later they pulled up a country western bar. There was a live show that night, and as people got up to dance, Milan shocked her by standing and holding out a hand. He actually knew how to line dance! Would this man ever stop surprising her? She certainly hoped not.

They closed the bar down, then walked through the streets of Vienna, stopping every now and again to window shop. Near their hotel, he pulled her toward a jewelry store. Ella tried hard to ignore it when she saw him look at a diamond ring, then glance to her finger, then back at the ring again. It was just the sort of ring she would have chosen for herself.

*June 10, 2012*

Ella opened her eyes and stretched, the smile from last night's encounter with Milan still playing on her lips. It had been perfect, except … as they said goodbye, she had sensed something in him—that conflicted feeling again. Well, she couldn't just wait for him to disappear on her.

Ella: My love, are you okay? I don't want to pry, but I feel like you are struggling with something. Can I do anything to help?

Milan: You never cease to amaze me. Yes, I have been feeling unsettled, and unsure of my direction. I used to know exactly where I was going in life. I always had a plan. Since I met you, that plan no longer seems to fit. I do not like the university where I am teaching, and there have been major changes in my other businesses as well. It will all work out—it always does—but I cannot see the way.

And then there is you—your life. I want us to have a future together, but I cannot forget that you are a mother. I think of your kids and how they would deal with all of this. I could not live with myself if I was the cause of any pain.

Ella: I appreciate your concern, and I love you for it. But

I can make changes and still be a good mother. Changes can come from both of us, not just you. Anyway, I'm here if you want to talk.

She pressed send; then, instead of waiting for a reply, she signed off. As much as she wanted to talk about a real future with him, she didn't know what to say when he brought up her boys. She could not deny that no matter how she and Milan came together in real life, Brent and Dirk would be drastically affected.

That night, she had the strangest dream; actually, it was more like a series of visions, almost as if she was watching a movie. In the first scene, she could see Milan playing hockey. He sailed across the ice as if he'd been born on skates, then slipped the puck right past the goalie for the perfect score.

A little bit later, she and Milan were in a parking lot, where they met up with two young men. They were both slim and tall, with black hair and very dark eyes. Milan hugged each of them, and Ella knew without a doubt that they were his sons Anton and Valy. Ella kept waiting for them to say hello to her, then realized that they couldn't see her! She was appearing in Milan's life as he had appeared in her kitchen at Easter. She followed them over to a car, an off-white BMW sedan, and watched as they got in. Milan rolled down the window, and she said she would see him at home. Smiling, he nodded that he understood.

Ella awoke with a start. This had been different than every other visit to him, but she couldn't place her finger on it. Suddenly, she burst out laughing, for she knew what it was—the feeling of home. In the vision, his home had become her home. Or was it just that wherever he was would be "home" to her?

Before going to work, she dashed off a quick note to him, describing the scenes and asking if he had known she was there, or if she was only dreaming. She also sent him a song:

"Feels Like Home," by Chantal Kreviazuk.

Milan: Yes! I was with my boys last night. We met some friends for dinner after my hockey game. Did I ever tell you I play hockey? I love it, but I have been too busy to play much lately. Anyway, later, at the restaurant, one of my friends tried to set up me up with his niece. He started telling me what a nice woman she is, smart and beautiful, and maybe I would like to take her to dinner some time. Without even thinking, I told him that she sounded lovely, but I couldn't go out with her because I'm already taken. Suddenly I looked over and Anton and Valy were staring at me in shock. They have not heard me say I was "taken" in a long time ... not since Ioana. They didn't say anything until we got back to the house, but then they asked me, who was this mysterious lady I had been hiding from them? So, my love, I wound up telling them about you—well, all except how we visit each other. I don't even understand that myself, so how could I explain it to them? They would take me to the nearest psychiatrist, I think. I did tell them we met on the game and have been communicating online ever since. That is common enough these days, especially with people of their generation. It felt good to finally tell someone about you, and I'm glad it was my boys. Now they have gone and it is time for me to get to work. All my love, Milan

*June 11, 2012*

Milan: Ella, my love … I just got home, after an awful day at work—back-to-back meetings and nothing resolved. I didn't even have time for coffee. I could not write you and I apologize for that. The next few days are going to be just as crazy. I have to be in Vienna tomorrow, then London on Saturday. By Monday, I'll be back here in Romania. There are big shifts happening in my company, and I will be deciding whom I want to continue working with. I will be in more meetings, hiring and firing people—never an easy thing.

So if you don't hear from me, don't think I am running. Please, baby, be patient with me. I love you so much! Milan

There it was again: be patient. Ella was trying, but she couldn't deny the feeling she got when she read these latest messages. First he had told his sons about her, now these changes in his company? Were Staci's predictions beginning to come true? It took all of her strength not to ask him.

The glimmer of hope was making it more and more

difficult to live with John. At first, it had been easy to compartmentalize her life. Milan was a fantasy; John and the boys were her reality. Now her worlds seemed to bleed into each other, and it felt more like an affair. She wanted desperately to just tell John that she had met someone else, but she had promised Milan that she wouldn't. Sometimes she would catch her husband giving her a strange look, as though he wanted to have a serious talk. If he did confront her about the rift in their marriage, she didn't know if she'd be able to lie. What's more, if Milan was serious about a future with her, why did he keep asking her not to tell her husband? She could not seem to shake this feeling of foreboding.

In the meantime, their trysts continued. Each night, they met somewhere in the ether, dining, dancing, and talking for hours. They talked about everything—their childhoods, where they wanted to visit and all the things they would do together "someday", when they were together in real life. And when it got too painful to think about when someday would come, if ever, they stopped talking all together and he would lower his lips to hers. Ella would wake up in her own bed, sweaty and exhausted and more confused than ever. She often felt like she was sleepwalking through her day, and she knew she was taking on Milan's stress at work. He hadn't elaborated on the reason, but he was always worried and exhausted.

Then one day in late June, she sat down in front of the computer to catch up on her own neglected paperwork when it beeped with a message. She took a sip of her coffee, opened up her email, and began reading the words that would change everything.

Milan: My dear Ella, I have been dying to write these words for so long, but I did not know how to begin. When we met, I thought I had my life under control. I had my work and my family, and if I never found love after losing Ioana; well, I had begun to believe that it was just my fate to be alone. Then I met you, and suddenly my own life no longer made sense to me. You are there, married with children, and I am here, with no desire to ever live in the U.S. I was offered several business opportunities over the years—lucrative opportunities—that I turned down because it would have required me to relocate to America. It has been incredibly difficult for me to accept that we communicate as we do, and very painful as well, and I can admit to you now that I often thought of ending our relationship altogether. That was why I disappeared for all those days back in May....

Suddenly short of breath, Ella minimized the screen and sat back. He was finally doing it—ending it for good. This was why he had never encouraged her to leave John; he didn't want to be responsible for breaking up a marriage when nothing was ever going to come of their tryst. She brought a shaking hand to her forehead and wiped the moisture gathering there away. She had been a fool, a patient fool, but a fool nonetheless.

She thought about getting out and going for a walk, a drive, anything to avoid reading the rest of his message. But in the end, common sense prevailed. She'd be alone in the house for several more hours, time to pull herself together before having to face her family. Besides, postponing the inevitable had never been her style. Slowly, she brought the mouse over, maximized the screen again, and continued reading.

Milan: Then something happened to me that changed everything—I dreamt of Ioana. Dreaming is a rare thing for me, you know, maybe because I sleep so little. But all of sudden there she was. We were sipping coffee and talking about our plans for the future, as if we had the rest of our lives together. Then suddenly she looked up at me and said, "But we didn't have that much time, did we? This is your second chance at love, Milan, don't throw it away." I don't know if this was a real message from her or not, but for me it changed everything. I still do not want to live in America, but I will do anything to be near you, and since you cannot leave your boys or take them from their father, I will have to come to you. I know I have been secretive about these changes in my companies over the past few months, and I love you for giving me the space I needed to work everything out. Well, I can tell you now that I have been restructuring my businesses so that I am no longer tied to Europe.

So what I have taken so long to say, my dear Manuela, is that I am ready. I am coming to America, to Seattle, to be with you. I can only pray to God that after all I have put you through, you still want this as much as I. All my love, Milan

# CHAPTER TEN

*June 21, 2012*

Ella strolled through the aisles of the furniture store, stopping every now and again to caress a brown leather couch or delicate lampshade. *Would Milan like this? It looks like the one in the London house ... perhaps not the same quality, though.*

It had become her favorite pastime, going to stores to look for things that she and Milan would use to furnish their new home, wherever that was. They had already decided they would look for a place within a reasonable distance from where Ella lived now and the clinic; that way she wouldn't have a far drive to work or to see her kids. *If,* she thought with a tightening in her gut, *they were even willing to see her when they found out.* She pushed the thought to the back of her mind, where she had been shoving all doubts associated with Milan's arrival.

When he had first written that he was moving to Seattle, Ella could scarcely believe it. "Thank you, God," she'd whispered, "Thank you, Ioana." For maybe Milan wasn't sure about the nature of his dream, but Ella was, and she truly believed that Ioana was guiding him from the spirit world. In his next note, Milan told her he wouldn't be coming until September, as he still had to wrap up his ongoing projects, close up his homes, and say his own goodbyes to family and friends. "You've been so patient, my love," he wrote, "Just be patient a bit longer and I'll be there, in your arms, for real." At first it seemed like a million years away, but when Ella thought about it, she realized he was right. They both needed this time to prepare.

So she was truly surprised when less than a week later, he announced that he had already told his family.

Milan: I have done it. Last night, at dinner with my family, I told them about you. I told them I was leaving for the U.S. I hadn't planned on telling them that way, but we were all sitting around, making small talk, and it suddenly seemed absurd to be keeping this secret from them. I swear, the room became so quiet it was as if I had suddenly turned the sound off! My father was especially shocked—I wish you could have seen his face. He knows how stubborn I am, and he had never seen me change my mind about something so big. When he finally does meet you, though, I'm sure he'll understand. :) You will have plenty of chances to meet him in "real life," as I will still have to go to Europe often for business. Then you and I will get to see Rome, Greece, all the places we've dreamed of.

Ella laughed out loud when she read the note, startling the three nurses sitting at the next table in the lunchroom.

Ella: I've been making my own plans, for your next birthday. I'm going to take you to Napa Valley, California. We'll spend the weekend in a romantic inn—bed & breakfasts, as we call them in the States. We'll rent a Vespa and cruise around the vineyards, stopping for wine tasting, cheese and crackers. We'll pack a picnic lunch and find a nice private place where we could make love in the sun. Of course, our room will have a bathtub big enough for two. The next morning we'll go on a hot air balloon trip over the valley. How does that sound?

Milan: Oh baby, this will be like a dream for me. I would be the happiest man on earth. I love you so much, Milan

For the first time, it began to feel real, and that day after work, she stopped at the first furniture store. It was a small, family-owned place and filled with eclectic things she had always wanted to buy but knew John wouldn't like.

John. She still had to tell John. The one thing she had always been adamant about was not cheating on her husband. She had stopped kidding herself a long time ago that what she was doing with Milan wasn't cheating, but the least she could do was tell him as soon as possible, and give him and the boys time to adjust before Milan arrived. Milan knew this, so for the life of her she couldn't understand his continued insistence that she keep their relationship a secret. "Once I am there," he wrote, "then you can separate from your husband, ask for a divorce.

Then we can get married and run away somewhere on our honeymoon ... anywhere you choose." She had no idea why he wanted her to wait, especially since he had already told his family, and she didn't ask. She told herself it was because Staci had counseled her to have patience and let things happen, but she knew the real reason was that she was afraid to hear the answer.

She did ask him about everything else, though. Did he have to find a job in Seattle in order to get a VISA? He told her that this was part of what he'd been setting up—an office for his company in Seattle—and that would be enough for a VISA. Eventually, of course, it would be a moot point, as they would be married and he would become a citizen. She also asked him what kind of wedding he wanted; she was picturing a traditional Romanian wedding. Her first wedding had been rather simple and nondescript, and she found herself looking forward to a bit of fanfare.

*July 1, 2012*

Milan: Ella, my love, I've been so busy all day, this was the first time I had a chance to write. Good news, though—I have a connection in the government who is going to help expedite my VISA. I will be there in mid-September. Good night and sweet dreams. I'm waiting for you to ring my bell. I love you! Milan

Ella might not have been able to tell John about Milan,

but there was someone she could tell. Besides, she owed Shelby a dinner anyway. She called her friend and asked if she wanted to go to their favorite place—a quaint cafe near the Puget Sound—the following Saturday.

"I'd love to!" Shelby exclaimed. "Do you mind if Allison joins us? We already had tentative plans for that night."

"Sure," Ella said, "The more the merrier, and I haven't seen Allison in ages."

"Okay…" Shelby paused. "Ella, is something going on with you? You sound, *different*."

Ella laughed. Different, now there is an understatement. "Actually, there is something going on, and I'll tell you all about it when I see you."

The day of their meeting, Ella was buzzing with excitement. Finally, she would get to tell someone in her life about Milan; well, someone other than a psychic. She trusted Allison and Shelby implicitly, and, even better, she knew Allison was fascinated by supernatural phenomena. When she arrived at the restaurant, her friends were already waiting. They all hugged, then Allison said, "Ella, you look amazing." She turned to Shelby, "You're right something is different." Ella just laughed mysteriously, then they followed the maître d to their table.

They got settled in and ordered their first round of drinks. "Okay, 'fess up, Ella," Shelby said. "Did you get a promotion?" Ella shook her head. "Change jobs?" Another shake of her head. "Have work done?" Ella raised an eyebrow at that one, then shook her head.

"New man?" Allison chimed in, and she and Shelby laughed at the absurdity of the idea. When Ella didn't join in, they looked over at her, mouths dropping, as she slowly nodded.

Just then, the waiter had brought their drinks. Ella took a few greedy gulps then started at the beginning. "I met him about four months ago, on this Internet game I'd been playing as a way to keep tabs on the boys." She took another sip, ignoring Shelby's look of surprise that she had been keeping a secret for that long. "Anyway, this man and I began to *dream together.* I would dream that we were together—you know—*sexually,* and the next day he would write that he had had the same experience." Ever since then, we have been getting together every night and it is like I can see the world through his eyes. He is in Europe, and traveling on business, and I am seeing all these wonderful places. It doesn't hurt that he is gorgeous, really creative and very sexy."

She paused, enjoying the look on her friends' faces; their eyes were glued to her, waiting for the next thing she would say. "Well … we have fallen in love with each other, and he is moving to Seattle!"

Shelby was quiet, but Allison breathed, "Oh my God! What does he look like?"

"I don't have a picture of him, but I see him clearly when we are together. He is tall with black hair and blue eyes. His skin is light, just a little darker than my own. He has a gorgeous body, nicely defined muscles everywhere. He is Romanian. He is multilingual; he can speak English, French, Spanish, German, Norwegian and Romanian fluently. He owns computer companies and has a few different homes—all beautiful. He dances well, and he is exceptionally romantic…" Ella trailed off for a moment, then caught Shelby's eye. "I didn't tell you until now because I didn't know if it was really going to happen."

"Tell me more about him," Allison pleaded.

"Okay, well, it seems he needs very little sleep, like an hour a day … Sometimes none at all."

Allison narrowed her eyes. "Hold on. You are saying he is Romanian, handsome, never sleeps, and he has seduced you over and over while you were in some kind of a hypnotic trance? He's a vampire!" She leaned far back in her chair and put her hands over her mouth, then came back and added, "Oh my fucking God, Ella is bringing a vampire to Seattle!"

Ella looked at her, trying to tell if she was serious. "But I don't believe in vampires. Do you?"

At this point, both Allison and Shelby shrugged their shoulders and said in unison, "I don't know."

The three of them sat quietly for a few moments pondering this while they sipped their glasses of wine.

Finally Ella said, "Ah shit. Well, I believe in ghosts and spirits, but I just have the hardest time believing in vampires. Even if he is one, I'm really in love with this guy."

Shelby had been unusually quiet, but now she leaned in toward Ella and asked, "What about John?"

Ella sighed sadly. She had expected the question, of course, but it didn't make it any easier to say the answer aloud, even to her friends. "I still love John, but it's a very different kind of love. We've been more like friends, or partners in child rearing, for years now. He doesn't make me feel beautiful or sexy. In fact, he tends to do just the opposite. Remember last December, when I was working out really hard? One of the personal trainers complimented me on how I looked. I went home feeling great, until I told John and he said the trainer was just trying to get a Christmas tip."

Allison made a sympathetic clucking sound and Shelby just nodded. It wasn't the first story she had heard about John over the years.

"And we never have sex anymore," Ella continued, feeling suddenly like she was pleading her case. "In fact, we never even talk—just hello and goodbye, mostly for the boys' benefit. It's only because of the boys that I've stayed for so long. I don't want to hurt them. I don't want to hurt him either. But lately I've begun to realize that keeping this marriage together is not good for any of us. It is keeping John from finding happiness elsewhere, and Dirk and Brent are going to have a loveless relationship as a model.

"Milan, on the other hand, makes me feel like I'm the most beautiful woman in the entire world. He has so much passion and desire...." Ella felt the silly grin split her face but was powerless to stop it. It felt so good to speak about him.

"He's a vampire," they said together. "That is how they are."

"Look, I know the teenage Twilight series was really popular, but do you really think there is any truth to all that?"

"I don't know," they said, again in unison and with identical smirks.

Ella smiled. "Actually, I did ask him early on if he was

a vampire. He said no."

Allison and Shelby laughed even louder this time. "Of course he said he wasn't! Did you really think he would tell you if he was?"

Shrugging her shoulders, Ella decided it was time for a change of subject. "So Allison, what's been going on in your life lately?"

Shortly after arriving home, she had another one of her visions. One minute she was sitting at the desk in her office, the next she was with Milan. They had just driven to his parents' house, a palatial estate in a very old, very affluent community. As always, he got out of the car and walked over to open her door for her, then offered her his hand. As they walked up to the home arm in arm, Ella was filled with the giddy anticipation that came from being an invisible observer of Milan's world.

A tall, slender, elegantly dressed woman answered the door almost before Milan rang the bell. Ella knew instantly that she was his mother, for the resemblance was unmistakable, from the jet-black hair to the piercing cobalt eyes. She grabbed him into a tight hug and kissed him on both cheeks. His father, who had walked up behind her, did the same, patting his son on the back.

As they followed his parents towards the back of the house, Ella took in the tasteful, clearly expensive décor and fell a little bit more in love with Milan. She knew his father had lost his job in 1989, shortly after the collapse of the Iron Curtain and the Romanian Revolution, and they would have lost everything had Milan not stepped in. He was little more than a child back then, but he was already earning money designing his own software. He had taken care of his family ever since, and although he had downplayed his contribution to Ella, it was obvious to her that he was very generous.

They entered a large, modern kitchen, where Milan's mother had just finished preparing a meal. As they sat down at the table to share a bottle of red wine, Ella studied his mother more closely. She looked to be around ten years older than Ella, but did not have one gray hair. Even more impressive though was her proud, almost regal, bearing that transcended the fine home and tailor-made clothes. Ella could easily imagine her as a beautiful gypsy with flowing hair and colorful robes.

Ella listened to them chatter on for a bit, and although she didn't understand a word of what they said, it was clear from their expressions that Milan and his parents shared a close bond. She was thoroughly enjoying herself, until, suddenly, his mother looked directly at her and narrowed her eyes. It was only for a brief moment, but Ella gasped, certain the woman had seen her. A few minutes later, Milan and his father got up to look at something in the garage, but Ella remained in the kitchen. As soon as they left, Milan's mother looked straight at her again. She made a cross with her fingers and held them up at Ella as she hissed out, "Leave my son alone! You have no business with him!"

With that, the vision ended. When Ella opened her eyes she was back in her office. "Uh, that was bizarre," she muttered to herself. "That woman treated me like I was a witch or something." It bothered her. Then she realized the thing that bothered her most was that *his mother could see her.* Up until that moment, she had really loved this invisibility game of theirs. *How could she see her? Was it some genetic ability that Milan and his mother shared?*

Whatever this was, she decided Milan didn't need to know about it. It would just freak him out. Maybe Ella has just imagined the whole thing. Still, she couldn't shake the awful feeling of foreboding.

*July 31, 2012*

Milan: Dear Ella, I cannot believe that I will be with you in a little over a month. But what a busy month it will be! I am travelling to half a dozen cities, then I am taking my first vacation in years—skiing in the Alps with a friend of mine. It is their farewell present to me before I leave them for "that American," as they call you. :) I will write more later. All my love, Milan.

*August 10, 2012*

As Milan had travelled throughout Europe settling his affairs, he'd taken Ella with him. They had been Paris, Holland, and Romania. "That's the way to my parents' home," he said as they passed the turnoff. Ella nodded but said nothing about being there before or her disturbing encounter with his mother.

Tonight, Ella was getting a tour of Copenhagen, courtesy of her personal and quite knowledgeable guide. She loved the way she could see everything so clearly and hear Milan talking to her as they walked around. She was once again invisible, and knew that every word she heard him say was actually a thought, rather than spoken aloud. Still, she relished their time together and looked forward to the day it would be real. He walked around and smiled at people, but otherwise appeared to be lost in his thoughts. That is what other people saw. Yet he and she were carrying on their own telepathic conversation, holding hands and taking in the sights.

They walked up and down Stroget, a wide street in the center of town. Stroget was a car-free shopping zone, and as Milan explained, the longest pedestrian shopping area in all of Europe. "That is the City Hall there," he said with a sidelong glance at the building, "and that over there is the King's New Square." Stroget was created in the early 1960s. Too many cars had started flooding the streets, so the city shut them out, making this a very successful area for merchants. Since then, other cities had copied the design.

She knew it was a little cold outside because Milan and all the other people walking on the street were wearing light coats and had their hands in their pockets, yet she couldn't feel it. In fact, she was perfectly warm and comfortable. Yes, there was a definite advantage to this kind of travel. She also noticed that in this dream state she could look anyway she wished—she had her college figure back and her hair and makeup were always perfect. She was still herself, just the best version.

He turned down a small street off Stroget and stood in front of a closed building. "This was once the famous Museum Erotica," he informed her. "It was a sex museum in the '90s, but closed a few years ago because the owner died."

"A museum of sex would have been great fun to see," she said, winking saucily. "Oh well."

Milan squeezed her hand, then said he was hungry, so they strolled down the street and found a restaurant called Noma. Milan thoroughly enjoyed a meal of fish prepared in a variety of traditional Nordic ways, and she thoroughly enjoyed watching him. "Next time, you'll try it too, my dear," he told her as they headed over to see the famous statue called "The Little Mermaid."

They were on their way to the Rosenborg Castle when Ella felt someone lightly touch her arm. She looked over at Milan, but he had his hands shoved into his pockets. She felt the touch again, more insistently this time, and when she looked down, she saw that it was John. She was back in her bed, and he was staring down at her intently.

"John, what the—?"

"You were dreaming, Ella," he said, looking at her with a strange expression. "You said something about a castle, and…"

"And what, John?" But even as she asked the question, Ella's heart began to race, because she knew what he was about to say.

"Who is Milan?"

A million things rushed her mind—a million lies. *He is a patient, a new colleague, the man who runs the grocery store.* She thought about Milan, begging her to keep this secret a little longer, and she thought of Staci, warning her to be patient. Then she looked into her husband's eyes and knew she could not live this lie a second longer.

"John, we need to talk...."

*August 30, 2012*

The apartment was smaller than she would have liked, but it was full of light and in one of the oldest, most beautiful neighborhoods in Seattle. It was not far from the clinic or the high school where Dirk and Brent would go, and it had an extra bedroom for when they came to stay. Besides it was the best she could get on such short notice.

The separation from John had been predictably polite and civilized. She had told him the abbreviated story of her relationship with Milan—that she had fallen for a man she had met online, and he was moving here. John would never have believed the truth, and although she didn't think he would do anything to hurt her, she wasn't willing to risk partial custody of her boys by sounding like a crazy woman. If John was shocked that she was leaving him for someone she had met on a computer, he didn't show it.

"Did you plan on staying in the house?" he asked, his tone matter of fact, but she could see the hurt behind his calm demeanor.

"No, we—I mean—*I* am going to look for a place. Maybe I can just stay here until I find—-"

"Yes, yes, of course," he cut her off. He moved into the guest room that very night. They lived like that for a week and a half, with Ella's guilt eating away at her every time she looked at him. A few times she thought he was about to say something, then thought better of it. *After all these years, he is not even willing to fight for me.* One day, she couldn't take it anymore; she called her real estate agent and told her to find her something—anything—suitable as soon as possible. A week later, she was all moved into the place she would share with Milan.

The boys had been surprisingly understanding about the separation from John, and why wouldn't they? As Dirk put it, all of his friends' parents were already divorced. Sadly, it sounded like her sons had been waiting for the day their marriage ended. Such was the world today.

And so she had moved into the apartment, mourning her past but looking forward to her future. She returned to the furniture stores, this time actually purchasing all the furniture and knickknacks she'd had her eye on the past few weeks. Shelby and Allison helped her decorate, and the boys even came over and helped her paint. And she didn't tell Milan anything that had transpired; let him enjoy his vacation without worrying, and when he arrived in Seattle she would surprise him with their new home. She just had to wait a few more weeks, and their life would finally begin.

On August 25, he wrote to tell her that he had booked his flight to Seattle, and gave her the time he landed and his flight number, "so she didn't forget to get him." Ella laughed out loud at that one. And on September 2, he wrote that he had finally finished up his business and was packing to leave for the Alps the next day. "I don't know how I'm going to concentrate on the slopes, knowing that I will be seeing you so soon. I cannot wait, my darling." He then told her that the Internet service may be sketchy there, but said he would write as often as he could. Ella wrote back, telling him not to worry, to enjoy and be safe.

She heard nothing from him for the rest of the week. At first she thought little of it; after all, he had warned her about the Internet connection. By the second week, she started to worry; surely he could have written her by now. She had never thought to ask for a phone number—how could she have been so stupid? By the third week, the week before he was to fly to Seattle, she had caught an awful chill that she couldn't seem to shake, despite the heat wave in Seattle. She shut off the air conditioner in the apartment and showed up at work in layers of clothing, which drew strange looks from her coworkers but did nothing to warm her up. A few people suggested she was coming down with something, but Ella knew better, and it terrified her. As soon as she had a few minutes, she ducked into the ladies room, pulled out her phone, and typed out a desperate message to him.

Ella: Milan, where are you? I have heard nothing from you in weeks, haven't felt anything from you except this horrible cold. Are you okay? I am terribly worried about you. Please write me—I am going crazy. Love, Ella

After work Ella went straight home, relieved that the boys were with John. They'd had enough upheaval in their lives recently and she didn't want to scare them with her "condition." Too tired to eat, she turned the heat up and slipped into bed fully dressed. Within minutes she was in a deep sleep.

*Ella, my love…*

Ella's eyes fluttered open. She had clearly heard Milan's voice, waking her up as he had done a million times before. Was he here? The room was dark, other than a stream of moonlight coming in through the window. Ella glanced around, gasping when she saw his familiar form standing on the other side of the room. Slowly, he walked toward her and sat down on the bed. He took her hand gently and she noticed his was ice-cold. His eyes inexplicably sad, he looked down at her for moment before pulling back the covers and sliding into bed with her.

The next morning, Ella awoke to an empty bed and joints so stiff with cold it was painful to move. Only the thought that Milan may have replied to her message gave her the strength. Wincing with the effort, she sat up, swung her feet over the side of the bed and headed over the computer.

*September 16, 2012*

Milan: My darling Ella, I've hesitated to write this to you. I know I am supposed to be there soon, but I cannot shake this feeling like something's going to happen to me before I can leave this place. Do you remember how I told you about my car accident premonition? It feels like that again, but this time I am not ready to accept my death, because this time I have you to live for. I have felt this way for some time; this is why I told you not to break with your husband, because I could not bear for you to be alone. I believe in God and we are all in His hands, so whatever will be, will be. No matter what happens, just remember that I love you, dear Ella, and nothing will stop us from being together—nothing. I hope this is just the rambling of a lonely man in a lonely place, and that I will see you in a few days. Until then, all my love, Milan.

As she read the words, Ella felt an icy chill running up her spine. She sat back in her chair and took several deep breaths. *Calm down, Ella, get a grip.* He came to you last night, he is alive. Then she remembered the sorrow in his eyes. Had he been saying goodbye? Ella forced the thought from her head and went into the bathroom to run the shower. She made the water as hot as she could without burning her skin, yet it still felt painfully cold. How was she ever going to endure another day of work like this?

Once at the clinic, Ella spent half her morning trying to stay awake and the other half making awkward excuses for wearing a scarf when it was ninety degrees outside. When it was finally time for her lunch break, she went to her office for a few minutes alone. She brought her hands to her mouth to blow on them and that's when she noticed that her fingertips were tinged with blue. She pulled out her hand mirror and looked at her face, her heart racing with fear. This could not be possible. She grabbed a tissue from the box on her desk and wiped off her lipstick. Her lips were blue as well! She walked over to the closet, got out her space heater and turned it on full blast, stretching her arms toward it in an attempt to warm up. It only made her feel more tired, as if she had been given a sedative.

"Dr. Rowen?" The sound of the voice jolted Ella awake; she must have dozed off. She looked up and saw Mary, the clinic's manager, standing at the door. "I could felt the heat from the hallway," Mary said loudly, "What are you doing?"

"I'm cold," Ella whispered faintly, her teeth chattering. Mary looked at her in disbelief. "It is a heat wave, for God's sake!" Then she shrugged her shoulders and moved on.

Ella didn't have time to be stung by Mary's brusqueness, for a new, truly awful thought had formed in her mind. She and Milan were so well connected; it was as if they shared one body instead of two. She was aware of many mysterious cases where people's hearts just stopped for no apparent reason. What if those people were linked to someone else the way she and Milan were? Did that mean he was turning blue, as she was? If he got so cold that his heart stopped, would her heart stop as well? If he died, would she die too? Ella could just imagine the scene—a young, healthy doctor, dead in her chair at work. At least her toxicology screen would be negative. She knew the conclusion of her autopsy would simply be: cardiac arrhythmia.

Then she had a new thought. If she was feeling his cold, then maybe he could feel the heater in her room; maybe it was helping him, wherever he was.

She started breathing slowly, thinking she could meditate and take a "look" around, but all she could see was a hazy whitish blue gray color. There was nothing else; no blue sky, no mountain peaks. It felt like she was buried under the snow, trapped. Suddenly Ella felt the walls closing in on her. *Calm down, Ella, just calm down.* She began breathing slowly again, telling her brain, "This is HIS freezing cold. This is not mine. I am warm. It is summer. I am warm." She said this to herself over and over and seemed to snap out of it. Her lips turned pink, and so did her fingers.

How could she help him? She truly had no idea where he was other than "the Alps." There are quite a few mountains there, shared by different countries. For the hundredth time, she chastised herself for not getting his number, or any of his friends' contact information. Shit, she didn't even know his last name!

She got on the computer and did a search for news stories on the Alps. Several popped up, all about the twenty feet of snow that had just buried the region. A wave of nausea swept over her. That was why she was so cold, why she felt like she was trapped. Milan was trapped under twenty sweet of snow! Was he injured—or worse? Had his premonition been correct?

Ella shook her head no. *Why would God bring us together this way, this crazy unbelievable way, just to tear us apart before we could even meet each other?* She refused to believe it, even when she did not receive a message from him the next day or the day after that. She refused to believe it when he missed his flight or when she read about additional news stories about the avalanche in the Alps, even after there was no Milan listed among the survivors.

*October 1, 2012*

Ella jumped at the sound of the alarm, even though she had been lying awake for hours. She could not remember the last time she had gotten a full night's sleep. She reached over and shut the alarm, ignoring the cell phone lying next to it. No need to check for messages these days. Her body felt heavy as she climbed out of bed and went to make coffee, at least that part of her morning ritual had stayed the same. As she went to get the cream, her gaze landed on the business card held to the fridge by a magnet. Diana G., Reiki Master. She ran her hand over the card, debating whether to call for an appointment. At least she had come highly recommended.

About a week after she learned of the avalanche, Ella had asked Shelby and Allison out for coffee. If she was being truthful, it was after Shelby had left her several worried voice mails. As they sat at the table at Starbucks, Ella fought to remain calm as Shelby told her to "forget the fraud," as she now called Milan. "I'm sorry, honey, but he was clearly just playing a game. He was never coming." Ella knew her friend's heart was in the right place, but this was not what she needed to hear. She knew Milan was alive—at least she thought she did—because she still felt him; still saw him in her dreams. Sometimes she would be swept with a sudden wave of sadness, or loneliness or fear, and knew it was coming from him. Shelby's words, while well intentioned, were tapping into her next greatest fear—that he had been deceiving her all along.

Allison remained silent during the conversation; then when they got up to leave, she fished a card out of her purse and handed it to Ella. "Go see Diana," she said, her eyes full of sympathy, "She will be able to help you." Ella nodded and took the card, too drained to ask whether by "help" she meant help her break the ties between her and Milan. She was not ready to do that.

Now, Ella took the card from the fridge and stared at it for a long moment before slipping it into the pocket of her robe. Maybe Diana could help her, but not to forget Milan. Sipping her coffee, she looked around the apartment she had decorated for them; then she sat at her computer and reread his last message, focusing on one line: "No matter what happens, just remember that I love you, dear Ella, and nothing will stop us from being together—*nothing*."

She would wait for him. If she had to, she would wait forever.

# DON'T MISS WHAT HAPPENS NEXT!

Malena is writing the sequel to this story, and you can be the first to know how things unfold. Go to www.MalenaPaltero.com to be notified of a very special pre-release event.

# ABOUT THE AUTHOR

Malena Paltero is an American author and a physician.

As a child, Malena became interested in reincarnation, dreams, and precognition. She was raised Lutheran and later converted to Catholicism. As she grew older and studied, she learned she actually identified best with the religious tenets of the Cathars, Celtics, Native Americans, and Indian religions. The majority of people in the world believe in reincarnation.

During her medical training, she felt that many of her colleagues believed in what was considered scientific, and they were quick to dismiss anything they couldn't see or hadn't personally experienced.

Malena feels that there is great emotional pain when death approaches for people and their loved ones who believe in one—and only one—lifetime. For people who believe in reincarnation, dying is just another part of living, and there is no fear. We are here to learn about love, kindness and compassion.

While preparing this book, Malena read material from many authors and researchers including Dr. Michael Newton, Dr. Brian Weiss, and Dr. Thomas Paul. There are books with compelling evidence about children who can remember their previous lives. Even more fascinating is that people with physical complaints in this life can be healed by, under proper care, going back and remembering previous lives. Through the spiritual interaction of its fictional characters, Blind Passion inadvertently touches upon the subject of past lives.

Blind Passion gives the reader a fun, exciting, and mind-bending story to read. It is truly a love story like no other.

Watch for the sequel to this novel in 2015.

CPSIA information can be obtained
at www.ICGtesting.com
Printed in the USA
FSOW02n0737030315
5427FS